We All Dance
at Once

Timothy J. Fuller

Cover art by: Dawn Normali
Cover design by: Tara Parente
Author photo courtesy of: Arthur Messal

ISBN-13: 978-0-9989468-0-1
ISBN-10: 0-9989468-0-X

www.runawaypoets.com

To Veronica, for the dance

In Japan for an international conference on religion, Campbell overheard another American delegate, a social philosopher from New York, say to a Shinto priest, "We've been now to a good many ceremonies and have seen quite a few of your shrines. But I don't get your ideology. I don't get your theology." The Japanese paused as though in deep thought and then slowly shook his head. "I think we don't have ideology," he said. "We don't have theology. We dance."

-Bill Moyers from the "Power of Myth"

CONTENTS

ACKNOWLEDGMENTS

I would like to thank the following people, either for their friendship, inspiration or support in some way or another on the road to publishing this manuscript: Nicholas Orso, Ryan Damian, Michael Vaz, Damon Lloyd, Liz Piren, Mike Hathaway, Mihir Shah, Alex Soudah, Marcia Rothschild, Gretel Bock, Michael Kineman, Wade Johnston, Arthur Messal, Kevin Reed and everyone on Team Inkwell. Without my family at the coffee shop I may never have understood the idea of "home," let alone found one. Also, a deep thanks to the citizens of Estes Park for not only accepting me into their community, but for teaching me what community is. Thank you Steve Nahaj for our beautiful collaborations and the continued enthusiasm. Thank you Ed Minus, not for teaching me how to write, but for nurturing a writer to become an author. Your undying support not only nurtured one, but allowed him to flourish in spite of nature's relentless adversity. Thank you Julia and John Fuller for raising not an author, but a good son. Thank you Benjamin Fuller, Jonathan Fuller, Daniel Fuller and Rebecca Fuller for teaching me to get along amongst the many and not only learn from them, but learn to love them. A heartfelt thanks to Leslie Kelley for the final edits and the final push to publish and to Faith Jones for convincing me to finally take a leap of faith. Also, to Dawn Normali for the cover art and to Tara Parente for the cover design. Sincerest gratitude to Rachel Hirshman and her son Eden for teaching me the healing transformative power of forgiveness. And finally, to all the women in my life, past and present, for your loving tenderness. For teaching my heart to be bold in battle, yet meek in triumph. Veronica, I'm sure you'll hear about this book someday, but I think you already know about it.

Author's Note

This book was written during the two years following the disclosed events, and I must state clearly here that these events have been fictionalized for dramatic purposes. During that time period I finished my undergraduate thesis, traveled back to Latin America and temped for a major French pharmaceutical company. Upon completing the novel I sent a hard copy to "Ana" and took off for Argentina with the intention of backpacking my way to Alaska over a two-year period. At that point I had no intention of publishing the manuscript; rather, I wrote it because the story was too good not to be written. I promised "Ana" during our brief time together that one day I would put it all into words, but obviously words always do a disservice to our experiences, especially of the more illumined sort that speak to our hearts and not to our ears.

The backpacking mission failed before it ever really got off the ground. I was having troubles before I even reached Bolivia and decided this wasn't the adventure I was ready for. I returned to the U.S. in 2011 and moved to Colorado. The story still haunted me and I wondered if I should publish. I found a job at a coffee shop and found a home in the mountains. It didn't seem that important anymore, I was happy and fulfilled. Years passed without much thought of the damn thing, but I still wanted to be an author. I attempted to contact publishers and agents with little success. Finally, with the thought of folding my hand I was encouraged by friends and family to just "put it out there." So here I am, reading over the work of a much younger self and seeing it with all the scrutiny of seven years of life experience.

I tried to dismantle it. I tried to add, subtract, multiply

and divide it. I scrutinized my characters and wanted to give them new words. I saw things my younger self never knew about and wanted to teach him the wisdom of an older self. However, playing with ecosystems is dangerous work. Add some rats to eat the mice and you might need a python to eat the rats. So, after much reflection and self-chastisement I've decided to let the chips fall where they did seven years ago and leave this as an honest testament to the experience as it was experienced. And perhaps in doing this it may represent the experience sincerely and not simply remain as a clever way to fictionalize myself into mythology, but rather speak of the naïve younger self and of his own wisdom, either romantic and foolish or courageous and heroic.

I hope my readers can see themselves in "Jack" and "Ana" and trace their own story through ours. And although our paths may not always converge but lead astray in thousands of new directions, entangled with thousands of new friends, acquaintances and lovers, we understand the ecosystems of ourselves are merely growing. With every fallen fruit a new seedling arises. Weddings are not always the beginning, just as funerals are not always the end. Take what you will. I'm still "Jack" and she is still "Ana." We are still alive and well, though apart, but our hearts still beat as one, one heartbeat heavy and strong.

-Monday, February 6, 2017 (Estes Park, CO)

It was some months after my first trip to Ecuador that my mind got off the beaten path and descended back down those dark corridors of madness. Since eighteen, I had been troubled by a mental illness that had been diagnosed depression with psychotic features, bipolar disorder, schizo-affective disorder, schizo-something-something...

I was attending Rutgers College at the time when the world suddenly became painted with a kaleidoscope of colors, seemingly normal things appearing absurdly significant, like puzzle pieces revealing a long-lost truth. I thought people could read my thoughts and send me messages telepathically. I sensed that I was the butt of the joke and everyone was laughing. I sensed aliens and alternate dimensions. I sensed the world was upside down. I sensed the world just wasn't right.

Needless to say, I was not stable and ended up back on medication and back on the local psychiatric ward. It was during those dim days of winter solitude that I was trapped, as though in a revolving door, with no hope of recovery and no hope of solace. Till that final visit to Lakeside Hospital when something occurred from the deepest place of all.

It was sometime in February that I had been up in my parents' house, bewitched by thousands of voices, voices of strangers and voices of friends, voices I couldn't even fathom and voices I couldn't even understand. I was assaulted to the point of no return, to the point where my thoughts became blurred with "their" thoughts, to the point where I had no thoughts of my own.

I trudged my disheveled 25-year-old self into my parents' bedroom, where I lay on their floor and moaned and cried and tore at my scalp and pressed my temples with my palms and cried some more and complained to my poor, anxious mother that there was no longer any hope. She explained the options. That I could struggle through this on my own and hope it improved, or I could go back to Lakeside and they could reevaluate my medication. And sensing the shroud, sensing the iron-wall of darkness all around me, I simply nodded and packed my bags.

They gave me an evaluation and admitted me back onto the ward. My mother looked teary-eyed and distressed. She looked the way I remember her when I was just a babe and in the hospital with a near fatal illness. She looked like I felt. She looked hopeless the way I felt hopeless. She looked dead the way I felt dead.

But then she gave me a kiss and a hug and told me, "Jack, you'll be alright, ok honey. Always have faith and you will never know despair, always have hope and you will never know darkness." Then she turned, just the way she had turned so many times before. The way she turned just after she had said goodbye. The way she would turn after she said the final goodbye. Just the way she had been turning her whole life and my whole life trying to assure us all that behind this entire shroud was a beautiful morning sunrise. That heart could melt ice. That heart could thaw the winter frost. That heart could raise the dead, if it needed to. That heart could bring you Eden if you let it.

And I strolled onto the ward, entombed in my own madness. I no longer had senses and no longer had thoughts. I had a body, but couldn't feel my body and wasn't even aware of my body. I had a brain, but it no longer worked. Memory disappeared, the past was dead and dark and silent. There was no future as there never could have been a future. And so in my mindless intoxicated stupor, they did all they could and dosed me heavily with Benzos. I walked around in an insomniac haze for two days before any rescue could be planned. I sat at the kitchen table and rolled an egg-yolk with

pleading eyes of mercy. I asked for justice with those pleading eyes, I asked the universe to shed a little grace. I sat in
plastic chairs and stared at blank walls. I lay in lifeless white
sheets and imagined the stars. I sat through art therapy and
hand-clapping aerobics. I sat in nothing and stared at nothing and imagined nothing at all, conscious of nothing at all
but the dancing dazzling circus show inside my own head.

Then finally came a night. Then finally came a night
when I had grown so weary that I trailed off to bed for the
first time in weeks, which seemed lifetimes and ages, until I
awoke to the shrieking sound of some sorrowful woman
moaning in her own particular stew of madness.

"NO! NO!" she shouted. "NO! Please, please someone
help me, PLEASE! Someone help!"

She sounded horrific. She sounded like the dead. She
sounded terrified just the way I felt terrified. Finally she
calmed as the nurses came to dose her even more heavily.
And then I began to calm and make a descent, possibly the
last descent, down to places that no man dares go, down to
an underworld no man dares imagine. I trudged through the
rooms of this haunted mind. I opened doors and saw ugly
faces. I looked through windows and saw beautiful faces. I
scoured the closets and heard the people of all the ages. I
unlocked cabinets and dresser drawers and heard eternity
and all its haunted people communing with me in all their
million languages.

And then something occurred which had not occurred
before. I sensed I was all alone, despite the crowded haunted
house, but then realized that we were all just communing.
And when this thought of unity occurred to me they quieted
and subsided and stopped with their clamoring and noise-
making and everything was silent. I went deeper, down the
rickety steps, down into the damp and dark basement. And
in the basement were some doors that lead to a deeper

basement. And I kept tunneling this way for a very long time, till I was no longer going down because down had now become up.

And as I rose I had the distinct vision that this was not me, but this was now God. That this thing God had taken hold, that all the world and all its mad people were in fact God, and they were now taking me to the heavens. And then up in the heavens I had a very distinct vision, a vision I will not forget and which could not be forgotten, a vision that reminded me of that first trip to the jungles of Ecuador. A young girl ambling about the forest, lost or forsaken. And she turned to me and said in her language, "Have you lost me again?" And I looked at her with those pleading sorrowful eyes and thought to tell her with my pleading sorrowful tongue, "Where have you gone now?" But, she just smiled a faint smile and said in a soft voice, "Know one thing, know one thing and you can find a way out." And just as I thought to utter the words she had drifted back into the jungle flora, back with the jungle fauna, back into the depths, back through the basement doors, back beneath the earth where I had always thought myself buried.

And as these visions came to fruition my fate was now coming to fruition. And in the darkness of that lonely colorless and tasteless and sense-less psychiatric ward I made a firm resolve that when I got out and when I was well again I would find my way to that jungle, I would find my way up and out of the basement, I would unlock the doors and the cabinets and the windows and the closets and chests and even the roof itself. And that house would no longer be a tomb. That house would no longer be my prison. That house would not be the end, but that house would be heaven.

We All Dance
at Once

Caught a ride off the coast early this morning in the hazy mist that envelops the Southern Manabí Province of Ecuador at this time of year, heading toward the main port city of Guayaquil several hours to the south. Many thoughts ran through my head, evoking a turbulence of emotions, both painful and joyous. I had been living in the small farming village of San Martin for the past six weeks as a student of anthropology, gaining valuable first-hand experience with the ethnographic method. Ethnography is all about adaptation, learning to live with a group of people and to see life through their eyes, to listen with their ears, to feel with their hearts. To be a good ethnographer you've got to overcome the nagging voice inside yourself that says, "Yes, I am an outsider, I have white skin and my accent is nearly intolerable, but will you have me?" No, that question won't get you very far because the people you live with actually appreciate that you're even interested in them at all. Well, after six brief weeks, which is all the program allowed, I felt myself beginning to think and feel as though I were a poor rural farmer. I could shit in an outhouse and take cold showers, farm with a machete and fight off the mosquitoes. But surely this was just a ruse invented by the novelty of my own imagination; I was no more a farmer than any gringo that visits this place. To my credit, I think by this time I had overcome that feeling of separation that detaches the casual foreign backpacker: I had shed any biases I may have been harboring and opened my eyes to a new kind of light.

But my sights were now turned to an entirely different ordeal, for you see my interests are disparate and unequivocally complex. During my first stay in this country just three years ago I became familiar with a certain indigenous brew used for its psychedelic and medicinal properties by the tribes inhabiting the Amazon. Ayahuasca has grown popular amongst the more bohemian sects of Western society, who use it in a ritual context to evoke visions and induce transcendental awe-inspiring insights into the more surreal nature of earthly existence. During that first stay in Ecuador I tasted the vine for myself, with little results, and left the jungle dismayed and cynical. But now, just three years later, I was on my way to Macas to work with the legendary Shuar shaman by the name of Emiliano Tséremp. The manner through which I discovered this man was as absurd as it was serendipitous.

While living on the coast I had befriended a drug dealer named Rodrigo who had been practicing for the past ten years to become a *curendero*, along with his amiable multi-lingual wife Gabriela. Toward the end of my stay he asked if I would like to participate in an ayahuasca ritual, and I responded with an unfettered affirmation. Was this not entirely insane! Surely this man was no saint, dealing coke and weed to backpackers from all over the planet; at times he could sound and act like a complete madman, ranting off about the tragedy of his wretched condition, but he was offering a taste of the divine and for that I could not deny his saintliness. Was this amateur *curendero*, this madman coke-fiend, this drug dealing lush going to inspire some source of all divinity within this creaky, unfit soul of a gringo? Surely it was not in my heritage to be imbibing psychedelic com-pounds grown in the deep recesses of the Amazon, but my spirit called to this vine of souls through the poetic majesty found in dreams.

Just several weeks prior I had been up in bed in my Ecuadorian "father's" concrete home reading about Daniel Pinchbeck's journey into the Oriente region of Ecuador to work with a shaman of the Secoya by the name of Don Ceasario. Shortly after finishing the passage in which his

4

visions are revealed I fell into a silent slumber beneath my mosquito netting voyaging off on my own inner vision quest. I was amidst an ancient tribe, surrounded by thick dense organic reality, snakes slithering from within the verdant orchestra of plant life, monkeys bellowing in the distance, when a fearsome shaman of ancient lore presented me with a small wooden bowl holding some thick awful concoction, which tasted as though the earth had been pureed into the most insidious brew imaginable. Soon after, I beheld the most beautiful, utterly fantastic scenery that one could envision: lofty panoramic views of deserts and oceans, ravines and mountains, waterfalls dropping down into gushing riverways winding about the valley floor. I was suspended in both time and space, floating thousands of feet above the earth as though my spirit had wrenched itself from that vile wasting flesh, and I was free to roam the earth without hindrance, without borders. I awoke startled in the dead of night to the sound of a loud "thump!" My "father" quickly turned on the light only to discover that my bed frame had fractured into pieces. We made swift work of repairing the bed, and I went to sleep that night certain of my destiny to find this enigmatic brew, to uncover the mystery and forge my own story with this ancient and powerful sacrament.

The night of the ceremony in Montanita, I met Rodrigo outside his house along the beachfront where dozens of young people were congregated around campfires, listening to loud techno music, drinking liquor and dancing beneath moonlight. His wife explained that we needed to purchase certain implements to help guide my journey, so we walked back to town to search for our necessary tools. After rummaging through a few local shops, we bought some scented wood, musky cologne, raw tobacco, and a bottle of water. Back at the house we prepared the tobacco juice and lit a fire along the center of the fenced-in compound encircling their home. Gabriela went to bed, along with her three small children, as Rodrigo and I prepared for the ceremony. I felt somewhat abandoned by the notion that she would not be joining us, that I would be left to the vices of this wild-haired Colombian, but this was a do-or-die scenario and our endeavor could not be disturbed by such sentimental attachments.

"Let's begin," Rodrigo announced at the stroke of midnight. Then he said a little prayer and bathed himself in the cologne, handing me the bottle, which I proceeded to empty along my arms, chest and face. Smelling quite fragrant, we inhaled the tobacco juice up our noses, which produced the equivalent effect of eating a jalapeno pepper. Sinuses cleared, we were prepared to ingest the brew, which Rodrigo cleansed with a ceremonial leaf and then poured out of an innocent-looking green soda bottle and into a wooden bowl. He quickly offered the medicine to the sky, and then choked it down with a bit of a harrowing look upon his visage, a sight that instilled within me one last regret for being so brash, so entirely idiotic. I too offered my bowl to the heavens, and then quickly swallowed the ayahuasca, shuddering at the awful taste of liquid wood. Soon, I thought, the drug would overcome me and I would feel the need to purge. I had checked the bathroom just one hour prior to make certain there was sufficient toilet paper, and as the drug settled in my system I was thankful I had taken such quaint precautions.

We sat there for quite some time, Rodrigo resting on a nasty old mattress and me seated by the fire, feeding the flames with small kindling. Soon enough I felt my stomach groaning with distress and yelled to Rodrigo, *"Necesito vomitar!"* I ran to the corner of the compound and puked up the contents of my stomach, including a half-digested pizza from just a few hours prior, when suddenly the effect of the drug overcame me with bizarre visions inscribed upon the soil. The countenance of angels and demons became markedly noticeable from within the earth; then as I gazed down at the pile of vomit, which at that moment I was unaware of being vomit, I envisioned the pile as a miniature Stonehenge, complete with tiny ant-people walking about the complex as they may have done thousands of years ago. I related the vision as best I could to Rodrigo, who replied with some enthusiasm: *"Este es un buen vision!"*

We commenced our visions along the mattress, as I noticed a loud hum from somewhere above, a sort of "wa-wa-wa-wa" sound. When I asked Rodrigo what it was he said, "The earth is composed of energy, as well as our bodies. What you're hearing is the grand motor of ourselves and of the universe." Then while I was staring at the tree to the right of me, its branches came to life, twisting and bending, throbbing and pulsing with unseen energy. I could sense this tree inhaling just like any other living being. Rodrigo was a genius! This plant reveals the true nature of the world! I was blind and now can see: this world is alive and I barely knew it! But soon enough I closed my eyes and let the visions overwhelm my senses. Fantastic geometric patterns swirled about me, diamonds and pentagons, twisting in the shape of a double-helix. I dislodged from my body and floated above the earth, as though in a dream, taking a ride on the magic carpet of Arabic myth. As I flew above the earth I noticed a fly buzzing about my ear, which I sought to kill with my hand, but then I realized that perhaps this fly had a message for me. Yes, these are all living things and now they can speak. "What do you have to tell me, good fly?" The fly said, *"Bienvenidos!"* and I broke out into a fit of wild triumphant laughter. This must be one of those Ecuadorian insects, yes: they've learned the local dialect despite their insectoid handicap. I greeted the fly with a welcoming embrace and continued on my vision quest into the unknown.

We drank again later in the night, with more vomiting, excreting, and the enchanting visitation of otherworldly reveries. I went to sleep that night dizzy and sick, hoping that when I awoke my senses would be back to normal. As I lay in Rodrigo's hammock, waiting to fall into a silent slumber, I thought hard about my plans for the next few weeks. Perhaps I should stay here and take more ayahuasca: after all, Rodrigo was practically a shaman in training, but some part of me felt obligated to get straight to the source, to work with the vine first-hand and study in a more natural setting. My dreams revealed very little that night, and when I awoke the world was still in disarray. I felt woozy with an upset stomach, everything spinning, like the most wretched hangover one could fathom. I lay outside on the ground for quite some time. Then Gabriela awoke and asked me about my experience the night before.

"Revelations for sure, but I don't know what to make of them."

"You're just beginning," she said with her gentle eyes of reassurance. "The first night is a process of cleansing. You will need a few weeks if you are to have any profound visions."

"There were visions, and lofty vistas, but I think I might be more suited to studying with an experienced shaman in the Oriente, if you know what I mean."

"That's your choice. If you want I can get in touch with my ex-husband living in Macas, he's a Shuar Shaman with forty odd years of experience working with the medicine. I could arrange for your meeting if you were so inclined."

I thought it through for a moment, the journey and the expense, but it felt absolutely right, putting to rest my apprehensions about traveling to Quito to book some kind of touristy shamanic retreat.

"That sounds perfect," I declared. "Can you get in touch with him this weekend?"

"I'll call him right now if you want," she replied, then picked up her cell phone and began to text. How utterly ridiculous, I thought, imagining this fearsome Shuar, dressed in a banana leaf skirt, necklaces of crocodile teeth draped across his broad chest, plumage of wild parrots sticking upward from his crown of feathers, perhaps hunting monkeys howling within the canopy, then bending down and picking up his cell phone and texting Gabriela from halfway across the country.

I spent some time that morning playing with the children, getting my head on straight so I could head back to San Martin with some semblance of normalcy. After a few hours we bargained down the price of the ordeal, and Emiliano accepted my offer to come visit by the end of the week. He mentioned that I would have to spend at least one week taking the medicine every night of my stay. Still hungover at the moment, I thought this sounded a bit unreasonable; I was beginning to question my motives, which were many and sincere, but inexplicable for sure. I accepted the offer and thanked Rodrigo and Gabriela for their hospitality, said goodbye to the young ones, then walked back to town to catch a bus up the coast to my family living in San Martin.

Riding along the coastal highway I admired the blue Pacific Ocean stretching out to the horizon. I began to ponder the coming weeks ahead. I had one week to make it to Macas, and I decided to plan a trip up into the Sierra before descending down the Andean Cordillera into the Amazon to meet with Emiliano. This was a strange story to say the least, getting stranger by the moment. I asked the ocean for peace of mind, and it replied with an ebbing tide of crashing white foam.

That was on Friday and it is now Monday morning. Just arrived in Guayaquil with a welcoming monsoon of swell-tering heat. I could not express myself properly in this climate and made short work of booking the first bus into the Sierra. I had decided to take a chance and visit a few places up in the mountains before I descended into the jungle. The first stop on my path was a rather large city by the name of Riobamba, a place I knew nothing about, had never heard of or bothered to visit. The heat was intolerable, but I felt a certain calm when I thought of the ride into terra-incognita, such a blessing to change climates in such a fraction of time. Bought a *batido*, a type of fruit milkshake, as I waited for my bus to arrive, then quickly paid my ten cents at the turnstile and found the one o'clock to Riobamba. Noticing the indolent and casual manner of my fellow passengers, I stowed my backpack in the luggage compartment then calmed myself with a cigarette, a Marlboro Red made with a loathsome South American tobacco, which when smoked properly in this 90-plus weather felt even more toxic than usual. Our bus didn't depart till one-thirty and I was beginning to feel a little out of sorts. I asked the lady next to me if this bus was indeed heading to Riobamba, and she gently reassured me with a calm and polite *"Claro que si."*

As we were winding our way out of the city, young entrepreneurs constantly boarded with packages of chicken and rice, boiled yucca, tamales wrapped in cornhusks, ice cream sandwiches, and treats of every sort. The poverty on the outskirts of Guayaquil was a heart-wrenching sight, vast shantytowns built of wooden planks and scraps of metal crowded along hillsides filled with trash and filth. How many diseases and how much sorrow must be harbored along this nasty stretch of road one could only ponder and feel his heart calling out in shame for indulging in leisurely travel while the world suffered in a chaotic duress of binding and ineffable pain. I felt bad enough as it was, with the heat and all, and decided to buy a popsicle from one of these local vendors, perhaps helping the local economy while alleviating this torrential downpour of sweat oozing from my pores.

After an hour or so of vast tracks of banana plantations and landscapes that resembled Vietnam or somewhere in Southeast Asia, we climbed our way out of the obtrusive heat, and the wind gliding across my face through the open window called out of a cool mountain climate. I beheld the rising Andes beckoning from a distance. The roads were of poor quality, some might say impassable, but our bus held strong as we forged our way along thousand-foot ravines, skirting cliffsides without railings or safety measures. I noticed the passengers about me making the sign of the Holy Trinity and I prayed to our Father, the Son, and the Holy Ghost that I might arrive in Riobamba in a single piece, avoiding my ultimate and untimely demise before I could meet Don Emiliano and understand the true nature of exist-ence. But reality, as it was, calmed my hesitations about taking the medicine, as danger seemed much more imminent on the outside as it ever is or can be on the inside. Perhaps I would go mad, but at the very least I wouldn't burn up in a fiery wreck in one of these gushing riverways along the valley floor. The truth was, however, there was nothing to fear. These drivers, although brash and sometimes hung-over, were of a rare breed, valiant warrior types that carried their spears in the form of a steering wheel. Never in my travels did I witness an accident along these formidable roads, and although I had heard tales of buses careening off cliffsides, I chalked that up to myth meant to scare off the gringos.

After several hours of passing through small mountain villages, gaining altitude at immeasurable rate, we watched night slowly creep in through the windows and the bus grew dark. My mind was at ease and I began to anticipate my arrival in Riobamba. I only had planned for a one-night stay and now that I was off on my own, away from my loving community along the coast, I was beginning to get lonely and in need of some conversation. My Spanish was functional but hardly fluent, and I couldn't possibly express some of the unwieldy thoughts buried beneath my ponderous countenance. Soon enough, we descended into a vast city of lights, and I thanked the lord for delivering us safely to our destination without incident and in such a timely fashion. I quickly grabbed my luggage and headed across the street in search of accommodations. Without much trouble I spotted a nice hotel that was offering rooms for eight bucks a night. My room was neat and comfortable with running hot water and cable television. I washed, dressed in my most presentable attire, and then ambled down the main stretch of road in search of food and companionship.

After much searching, ducking in and out of all the local cafés, asking prices and comparing meals, I sat down at a quaint little establishment tucked a few paces off the main stretch. The room was pleasant, yet unadorned, empty of customers except for a lone gentleman dressed in suit and tie and carefully watching the nightly news as he sipped his potato soup. A young woman, obviously of Indian descent as evinced by her dark skin and high cheekbones, took my order and offered me some juice. After she returned from the kitchen she sat down in one of the booths and continued with her studies. She was an attractive girl, and I was interested in knowing what she was reading, but my shame-filled, introverted character along with my vivid and uncompromising imagination played out a multitude of objectionable responses to my inquiry. I could see the soup being thrown in my face, scalding my skin as if it were even that big a deal. But what's worse is that I couldn't tell if she spoke

English, and I obviously couldn't put up much conversation in any other language, so I refrained for the moment from approaching her table and sat there patiently awaiting my dinner as the businessman quietly flipped channels. Soon enough she was back from the kitchen with my meat and rice, brandishing an amiable smile and a seductive gaze, wishing me a pleasant meal.

As she sat back down in her booth I thought over the million ways I could approach her without sounding terribly idiotic or patronizing, but the longer I thought it through the more complicated the situation became. She glanced over at my table every so often, as I continued to absorb myself in dinner, never once letting her take notice of my interest. Soon enough my meal was through, and my obviously demoralized ego was going to let this woman pass by like so many others. She finished her studies and headed out the door onto the street, and I sat sulking as her mother cleared my table and offered me some coffee. I accepted, patiently waiting for her return, but to no avail. This was not going to be my conversation for this evening.

I donned my jacket and hat and headed out the door in search of a place to drink and possibly meet some fellow travelers. Along the way, not far from a local park, I noticed an internet café offering extremely reasonable rates, I think somewhere near twenty-five cents an hour, so I thought of emailing my younger brother Dylan to inform him of this monumental excursion into the Amazon to work with aya-hausca. As I sat down in the dark-lit café, another attractive young Ecuadorian woman peeked out from beneath the glare of her computer screen to greet me with a friendly smile. I smiled back and sat across from her as I logged onto my Gmail account to check my messages and write my brother.

Dear Dylan,

Just arrived in Riobamba, a large city up in the Sierra. To-morrow I'll be heading into Banos, the last stop before Puyo, on the edge of the jungle. I've arranged to work with a shaman in Macas, about four hours south of Puyo, for a period of 7 to 10 days, depending on how much money I have left. From what I've heard from my friend in Montanita he's one of the most experienced and well-respected men of his trade. I've haggled the price down to 70 dollars a day and he wants me to drink ayahuasca every night of my visit. I'm extremely excited about learning from ayahuasca in the jungle with an experienced shaman. Perhaps he can help guide my visions and heal my scarred psyche. I'll write you again once I return from Macas and let you know how the trip went. Until then wish me luck and perhaps I'll encounter you in my visions to come.

Love, Jack

As I wrote to my brother I occasionally sneaked a glance from around the computer screen, admiring the young woman so entirely absorbed in her monitor. Slowly, taking courage from my pitiful performance over at the café, recalling with a scornful malicious smirk my unmanly weakness, I worked up the nerve to ask the young woman a friendly question: "Excuse me Miss, do you happen to speak any English?"

She smiled and politely responded, "Yes, what can I do for you?"

"I was looking for a place to get a drink; do you know where that might be?"

"Yes, right out this door and walk down a few blocks; you'll find a few places that should still be open."

"Thank you, Miss. I was wondering, would you like to get a drink with me? I'm here all alone and could use the company."

She hesitated for a moment and looked down at her screen as though she had some unfinished business to attend to.

"I'm sorry," she responded, "but I don't drink."

"Coffee then? Would you have some coffee with me?"

Once more she hesitated, looking down at her screen, and then politely realigned her gaze with mine. "It's a little late for coffee, don't you think?"

"Well, hot chocolate then, or maybe a banana split or a five course meal if you happen to be hungry. I'm just looking for some company and you have very kind eyes."

Slightly abashed, her lips curved upward, as her chin pivoted on her right hand, glancing down at her screen and then back again. I figured a woman like this probably heard a compliment like that a thousand times a day, piquing my curiosity and pressing me forward.

"I should be done here in about one half an hour, is that alright by you?"

"Great! Fantastic! I'll be back in half an hour."

She smiled back, as I left the café and headed back to my room to dress a little more appropriately and get my head on straight. Soon enough I had made my way back to the café just as this lovely young woman was finishing up her business.

"What were you writing?" I asked as we ambled out the doorway.

"Nothing really, just surfing the internet as you say in America."

"Could you tell, was it really that obvious? Cause some people mistake me for European, but typically not Europeans. But I'll take that as a compliment, I'm very fond of my country and we do indeed like to surf the internet."

She laughed a little, I think she was laughing at me and

not with me, but I took that as a sign that maybe my quirky mannerisms might pay off.

"There's a coffee shop down a few blocks, might be open at this time of night."

"Hey, coffee's all coffee with me, I'll take what I can get."

She politely put out her hand in front of me and said, "Don't walk so fast, there's no rush, we'll get there when we get there."

"I'm sorry, it's not the coffee, I could take it or leave it to be honest, but I tend to walk a little faster than your average Latino."

"Are you implying that we're lazy and slothful?"

"No, not at all, I'm just implying that you walk impossibly slow."

She laughed as I purposely slowed my pace in a facetious manner, then she increased her pace in the fashion of a parody, which I found hilarious. Then we both resumed normal walking pace, and continued our conversation.

"So, I noticed it's cold here this time of year. Is this your winter or is your summer really cold?"

"Actually scientists have declared that we have four seasons, but this is still summer, it gets cold at night, but during the day it can get extremely warm."

"So, do you have an autumn? Because this feels like autumn."

"Trust me, when the sun is out you'll break a sweat."

"I don't want to break a sweat; I actually find this climate quite comfortable. By the way, your English is immaculate. Where did you study?"

"I studied in school since I was a young girl, but I'm taking courses right now at San Francisco University."

"Good for you; it's always good to encounter a local that can speak my dialect. To be honest, people like you are few and far between in this country. You're like us Americans,

16

satisfied to just get by while the rest of the world goes on speaking three or four languages at a time."

"Well, thank you, I guess; knowing English can bring opportunities. I'm hoping to get a position with the Embassy in Holland, and they require you to speak English."

"Shouldn't you know Dutch instead?"

"Is Dutch a language?"

"Yes, it's the language spoken in Holland, shouldn't you know that?"

"I thought the Dutch were a people?"

"Yes, and the Dutch speak Dutch!"

"Oh well, no chance of me learning Dutch, but they do require English."

"Well, you speak it very well."

"Thank you, I practice very hard."

"Is this the coffee shop you were talking about?" I asked as we passed a café with a closed sign.

"Oh shit! Look over there, across the street, that yogurt shop serves coffee, and I think they're still open."

We walked across the street and entered the yogurt shop, a kind of fast food ice cream place decked out in bright yellow, brilliantly lit up in a sort of dizzying Las Vegas kind of way. I ordered a coffee, and asked this young woman what she would like.

"Actually, I'd prefer a hot chocolate if that's alright."

"Sure, it's your money, right?" I jested.

"Of course," she replied, "I completely forgot that chivalry was dead."

"No, it's not dead, just slowly dying," I joked, "but I think its time we revived it, so consider this fifty cent hot chocolate on me."

"How kind of you, sir, you're so generous. How will I ever repay you?"

"You can start by telling me your name, that should

cover the hot chocolate."

"Ana Mendez, nice to meet you..."

"Jack Fields," I stated as I shook her hand, "at your service."

We sat down at one of the metal tables and I finally got a good look at my female companion. Her wavy dark hair rested gently along her slim shoulders, and her high cheekbones, like those of the Indians, accentuated her large dark eyes beneath arched brows. She had the brown skin of a *mestiza*, with thick red lips like those of a freshly cut fig. She was like a misplaced model who had never learned not to be humble. I felt myself become more nervous than usual at this moment, for I had not been aware when I had met her in the dark corner of the internet café that she was entirely out of my league.

"And what does such an educated woman as yourself do for work here in Riobamba?" I asked with some hesitation.

"I run a family business along with my mother, I studied as an engineer and now I help her raise chickens."

"Do you engineer the chickens?" I quipped.

"A smartass, eh? No, but I engineer their feed," she said as she took out a small notebook covered in numbers with decimal places and special signs that I could not comprehend.

"I didn't mean that as an insult, I've always admired those in the production of farm animals. As a matter of fact I always intended to raise my own, but I don't think I would ever be able to chop off their heads. I was actually a very strict vegetarian for several years in my youth."

"And what happened?"

"I grew weak."

"And so you learned to chop off their heads?"

"I learned to accept that someone was going to have to chop off their heads, that much I could deal with."

"Well, we only raise them, we don't kill them, but I see nothing wrong with taking life to sustain life, it's just the way things work."

"Yes, but it certainly is cruel, don't you think so?"

"Cruel? Perhaps, but life is cruel, don't ever think otherwise."

"Yes, but in its cruelty something beautiful arises, life is taken and life is sustained, the world thrives on a wildly unfathomable web of interconnectedness. One day you're a drop of water, the next you're the petal of a flower. We die a thousand deaths, but live for an eternity."

"And what is a philosopher doing here in Riobamba, are you seeking answers you couldn't find in America? Or are you merely here to ride the train to Devil's Nose?"

"Well, first I didn't know you had a train, or that there were any trains in this country for that matter. And second, I had no idea Riobamba existed until yesterday before I left the coast."

"So let me guess," she said in the highly unusual articulate manner that I was slowly growing accustomed to, "you've come here in search of the exotic, you're touring the countryside in search of raw experience to refine your senses and instill some kind of character in your deadened American psyche. You found your job dull and came seeking adventure, you saw the Pacific Ocean and marveled at the magic of its ebbing tide lapping up and down the empty coastline stretching endlessly without boundaries. You're on your way through the majestic Andes Cordillera to descend into a wild untouched virgin jungle to see monkeys bellow like madmen, and snakes that could eat a man alive. And now you've found an attractive local girl to fancy for an evening and tell to your friends back home--and you're asking yourself, how do I get this girl in bed?"

My lip unhinged and hung a bit lower than usual, my

salivary glands producing more moisture than I'm accustomed to. My eyes opened, my heart leaped up into my throat, creating fantastic vibrations that I wasn't even aware existed within the human body. I looked into the dark depths of her wide, glowing eyes and felt this strange connection with the human heart. Was this just some serendipitous encounter, or was this fate? Had I been traveling in the dark for ages, only to open my eyes and discover that it was destiny all along? Or perhaps I had stumbled off the beaten path and run up against a pebble that had twisted my ankle in a strange place that I would notice for an instant before I could regain my balance and realign my gaze.

I wasn't sure how to reply, but felt this silence growing more than awkward if we weren't to end with a kiss.

"Actually, I'm a student of anthropology, the study of human beings past and present. I was enrolled in a field school on the coast where I lived in a small farming community for six weeks. And yes, my spirit is dead and I'm seeking adventure, I'm seeking warm sunshine and fresh air, friendly glances from unusually attractive girls, cheap food and cold beer, dances that shake the hips at impossible angles. You understand a good deal about American backpackers, but I don't think it's in your capacity to understand me."

She smiled a little and took a sip from her chocolate drink, then looked at me beneath those exquisitely arched eyebrows, and asked, "And what's your mystery?"

"I'm a complicated man. I mean, I share a lot with just about every other foreigner that comes stumbling through here, but it was not my intention to get you in bed and saunter off into the next sunset to see just what other adventures await me beyond the horizon. I was lonely on the ride here from off the coast, leaving behind the only community I ever really knew, and as I approached you at

20

the café I was seeking companionship, another person who shared my language, not a cheap thrill to chalk up on the board of experiences to be had before I turn thirty. You looked friendly so I tossed a pebble to see just how far it would skip, and if you want to continue talking, I could use the conversation."

She laughed slightly and smiled warmly, then got up from her chair and said, "Well, you picked the right pebble."

We got up from our chairs and zipped up our jackets, emptied our drinks and ambled out into the frigid mountain air. We walked quietly for a minute down the hillside to a large empty park, filled with pathways through large expanses of grass and pond.

"This is Guayaquil Park," she announced. "This is my favorite place in the entire city. I come here on Sundays to see the children paddle their boats across the pond, to watch the men and women exit from the soccer matches down the street. At night it is dark and quiet, and if one sits by the water and listens carefully, unmindful of the biting cold, the human experiences of the past echo from the depths and a patient smile will bear any burden the day ahead could possibly have in mind."

"That's beautiful," I said as we walked casually side by side. I gently took her hand and held it softly as she turned and smiled.

"I find the greatest solace in the moments around action, and at night, just before my mind grows weary and I wander off to bed, I find it pleasant to slip out back behind the house and look at the moon and admire the stars. Without the celestial objects there would be no great joy in looking towards the heavens, but without the millions of dark spaces in between there would be nothing admirable in the stars themselves. I find the greatest joy in the silence between words, like the dark between light, it's the space that holds the fabric together that helps us distinguish one word from another."

We quietly held hands for a moment strolling aimlessly about the park. The lights surrounding the pond lit the way as we circled around the concrete pathways. I wasn't sure how this was all going to end, I could tell we shared a bond, but it was no longer my intention to just get laid, as I was certain it was not her intention to let that happen. My plan was to leave in the morning for the town of Banos, the last stop in the Sierra before the road descended into Puyo on the edge of the jungle. I was sure I had to be in Macas by Friday to meet with Emiliano, but sometimes, usually every several millions of years, a mountain emerges from the depths of the earth and no longer can we see from ocean to ocean without admiring the impossible handiwork inscribed with such tremendous potential.

All I knew at that moment was that I didn't want it to ever end, I wanted to inch forward at the pace of a three-toed sloth if necessary, to never get anywhere and to never want to get anywhere. It was the first time I had ever felt that way after holding a girl's hand, but for some reason her slender and refined fingers were better at holding my grasp than any lofty vista could ever move my soul. I wanted to write poetry, I wanted to bathe in the pond and make love beneath the stars, I never wanted to leave that park, even if I was old, crippled, and incapacitated by an accident I had sixty years ago. But the truth was that time, as cruel and ineffective as it is at retaining those aspects of life we deem most worthy, passed as swiftly as the single flap of a hummingbird's wings, and we had circled the park and were on our way back up the hillside before I could even express the most treasured sentiments that stirred in every corner of my heart.

We soon arrived at Ana's car and it was time to go our separate ways, each to our own home, our own beds to dwell in dreams. I was about to say my appropriate goodbye when she asked if I could use a lift.

A bright smile, from my toes to my lips, eased the loneliness I felt stirring on the horizon, and I accepted in a single affirmation that indeed sometimes a stone isn't just a stone, and if thrown under the right conditions at just the right angle it might just skip a little bit further than we had anticipated.

I directed her back to my hotel, and then reached out for a hug.

"Listen," I said, "I wasn't really planning on much for tomorrow, and I don't know what you had planned or might be planning. I don't know if you have work in the morning, or if you have to run some errands, but I really would like to see you again before I leave, and if you wouldn't mind being so considerate as to show me around, I wouldn't hesitate to accept."

She paused for a moment, then nervously gripped the steering wheel, "I have to meet some people tomorrow morning, early on, you know, business matters. But I'm off from school and don't have much to work on, so if you want to take a ride I suppose I could pick you up around ten or so, that is if you don't have any plans."

"No, not at all, that would be wonderful! Ten o'clock, right? I'll wait right out here by these steps. Well, it's been a wonderful evening and I look forward to seeing you tomorrow morning. Have beautiful dreams and if you don't show tomorrow at ten I'll just keep on waiting."

"Don't wait forever, some things take longer than forever!"

"And aren't those the best things to wait for?"

"Goodnight!" she said.

She made an illegal U-turn at the stop sign and sped off in the opposite direction, back to her mother's home, I supposed, where hundreds of clucking chickens waited to be fed. I, however, went to bed that night in my eight-dollar hotel room in complete and total silence, naked, yet to be born. The single thought that occupied my mind was the bus that departed from the Guayaquil station, the one o'clock that I mixed up with the one-thirty. Now, if I hadn't gotten on the wrong bus, if I hadn't been so busy smoking that loathsome Marlboro Red, a series of events might not have unfolded just the way they did. And that got me to thinking about this whole damn trip and the whole pattern of events that shapes and molds the human experience. Perhaps, I thought, sometimes we're meant to miss a bus ride or two, and when we do the world looks a bit different than it did before or since. To be right about it, this time it looked about thirty minutes different and I was glad it did.

I awoke in the dead of night in a dark and inhospitable room with an aching pain in my abdomen and a slightly enlarged left testicle. It was the kind of pain I had experienced in college before I ever had surgery to treat my varicocele, an abnormal enlargement of the vein that is in the scrotum and drains the testicles. It was a pain that came with sexual arousal, something I hadn't felt in a while, not since I recovered from the surgery and in light of my lack of partners over the past couple of years. But the fact of the matter remains: I tend to jack-off more than the average man my age and yet I felt no pain under such circumstances, and suddenly the dream which had startled me awake came to the forefront with great clarity.

There was a girl I had been infatuated with since before I can remember, perhaps since the first year of high school. She was, as far as I was concerned, the most beautiful girl I had ever seen, not only intelligent and talented beyond measure, but she also returned my glances and ack-nowledged my presence. She was a year ahead of me, but we took several classes together, including statistics and photography, and traded glances under the gaze of God at the Roman Catholic Church of Saint James. In this particular dream we were both at work in the darkroom in the lower level of the graphic design workshop, enlarging our photo-graphs without speaking a word or acknowledging the other. When I turned to say something and realized we were both grown adults, suddenly my timid awkwardness no longer seemed relevant and I leaned in and kissed her on the neck. Expecting a harsh and unforgiving slap in the face, I was astonished when she responded by kissing my lips and gently massaging my pants. We began to make out when the darkroom opened and the teacher entered only to behold me with my pants down to my ankles and no girl in sight. My startled fright came from the shock of sheer embarrassment and bewilderment because of the missing girl, and my enlarged left testicle apparently was the end result of merely dreaming about jerking off. How pathetic, I thought; not only do I not get the girl of my dreams within my actual dreams, but I incur real-life male ejaculatory problems while dreaming about masturbation!

I went to the bathroom sink and got a drink of water to wash down some aspirin, hoping it would cure my testicle problem and relieve some of the aching pain in my lower abdomen. I lay in bed but had trouble falling back asleep, not because of the pain or remembrance and fascination with the dream, but because I was so utterly and fantastically excited about tomorrow morning when I would reunite with Ana to uncover the passing of last night. I only hoped I hadn't made such an ass of myself that she would hesitate to show. But I had to come to understand that sometimes things happen for a reason, and sometimes the reason is the very thing that happened. If she chose to renege on her promise I couldn't hold a grudge or spiral into despair. After all, it seemed a likely outcome, but I still could acknowledge the circumstance and admire the beauty in the moment we shared. Thinking these thoughts calmed my nerves, and as the aspirin kicked in, a dark silence consumed my senses, the pain subsided and I drifted off to sleep.

I awoke the following morning with a clear head, a left testicle slightly diminished in size and appearance. I took a hot shower, shaved, brushed my teeth, dressed adequately for what I thought would be a frigid afternoon, and then strolled out the hotel door in search of coffee and food. The first establishment that caught my interest was owned by a disgruntled gentleman serving meat, bread and rice for breakfast. When I asked if the bread came with butter, he impolitely turned his head in disgust, and said, "It's a dollar fifty, you get meat, bread and rice! No butter! You can buy butter down the street!"

I passed on the buy-your-own butter deal and went searching for that nice little café where I ate last night. When I entered the attractive young waitress from the night before greeted me with a warm smile and asked if I would like breakfast.

"Yes, I'll have my eggs scrambled and my coffee black."

"Sure," she replied, "I'll be right back."

She danced her way back into the kitchen as I thought about the oddity of my pitiful performance here last night. Why was I so intimidated by these women when for all I knew I would never see them again? But suddenly, success with one called for success with another, at least on the approach side of the equation; the other half could only be figured out with time when I discovered all the variables. When she returned with my coffee, I politely smiled and began my introduction. "I saw you here last night reading a book. Could I ask what you were studying?"

"Oh yes, you were here last night. I was reading a novel by Gabriel Garcia Marquez, *One Hundred Years of Solitude*."

"Is it about a really lonely man?"

"It's about a lot of lonely men, but then again, isn't everything?"

"Even television?"

"Television is about millions of lonely people pretending not to be lonely."

"No, television is about selling millions of lonely people lonely things that will make them feel not so lonely."

"So, you agree?"

"I agree that the world is a lonely place."

She paused for a second and looked over at the few folks gathered around the other tables watching the television or reading the morning paper.

"Would you like butter with your toast?"

"Do I have to walk down the street to buy it?"

"No."

"Then yes, I will have some butter with my toast."

Then she smiled politely and quietly danced her way back into the kitchen to prepare my breakfast as I sat and watched the television, pretending not to be lonely while barely understanding a word of it. But the truth of the matter was that I wasn't as entirely lonely as one might think. I felt a nervous excitement throughout my body, a soft shudder of pure exalted energy from the base of my tingling spine and across my face, where a soft grin would not subside and my bright eyes would not blink. In just a few hours the dark alluring young woman whom I had shared hands with the night before would pick me up in her bright red pickup truck to introduce me to Riobamba, the very same city I had never cared to visit for more than a night, when out of all the places in the world it was the very place that I should have cared to know.

My obsession with the vine of souls, my trip to the jungle to work under the tutelage of Don Emiliano had ceased to occupy my thoughts as they had the day before, while my experiences along the coast seemed a faint memory of a forgone era. I could not rationalize this quirk in the fabric of my memory, but sometimes a day or even an hour can retain more value than years or decades of fruitless labor, relationships forged and folded, jobs worked and completed, books read and reread, aspirations sought and realized. At the moment I was entirely consumed by the infinite potential of the present, I noticed things that seemed incidental, like the napkins folded into perfect right triangles and the shapes and patterns created by the cream in my coffee, like stars born, galaxies imploding and exploding over and over, telling the story of the universe from that single point of boundless energy and, more importantly, of the potential yet to be destroyed.

I would have liked to compliment myself for my sage disposition, as though I had reached enlightenment from years of meditation, but the truth is not the truth when told by our own tongues, only when recounted by some neutral third party. No one could recognize this, of course; in the eyes of the external world I was merely a mute foreigner enjoying his coffee, pretending not to be lonely while watching the morning news. After some time my waitress returned from the kitchen with my eggs and toast. I thanked her politely and smiled with appreciation.

"Enjoy your vacation," she said.

"Enjoy your book," I replied.

Then she sat down in her booth and continued to read about the lonely town of Macondo, as I sat enraptured in the surreal nature of external reality, passively awaiting the arrival of each moment, and never expecting anything more than the moment before. I finished my coffee and left some change on the table, strolled back to my hotel and arranged for another night's stay with the concierge.

When ten o'clock arrived the sun was well above the horizon and the air was warm. I discarded my sweater and waited for Ana on the concrete stairs outside the hotel. As several minutes passed I began to worry. I lit a cigarette and watched it turn to ash. Fifteen minutes elapsed, then thirty. I was beginning to accept my fate, the fact that she would never arrive and I would be forced to go it alone. My eager excitement was slowly diminishing to despair as I watched each red truck speed by without stopping. Then, just when hope seemed lost, Ana pulled along the curb and waved out the window. I smiled and hopped in the passenger seat.

"How are the chickens?" I asked

"The chickens are fine, I'm sorry I'm late, but I had a few business matters to attend to."

"Selling eggs?"

"Kind of."

"Well, where are we heading?"

"I want to take you to the Ecological Park," she said as we sped down the main strip. "How much time do we have?"

"As much as we need, I already booked my room for another night, Banos can wait."

"Banos is nice, the waterfalls are pretty, but I think once you get to know Riobamba you will find its faults charming and its charms without faults."

"You were right about the sun; I think it really is summertime here."

She laughed as she looked at my sweater, then smiled nervously as she switched gears.

"I don't know what it is about you, but I feel all giddy, like a young school girl around her first real crush. You make me nervous, but you seem strangely familiar, are you sure we haven't met before?"

"Have you ever been to Jersey?"

"No, what's Jersey?"

"Probably not."

"You don't seem as American as you look."

"Do I really look all that American?"

"I mean your whole attitude is very Latino, like you don't have a care in the world, instead of racing against the clock. How long have you been in this country?"

"About six weeks, living with the farmers of San Martin, my "father" Don Vinicio and his loyal wife Maria. I feel very connected with this country, there's something so magical about the spirit of the people here. I've come across some impoverished men and women struggling to earn a day's pay, and although they toil and perhaps suffer in a way I will never truly understand, there is magic in their suffering, a polite and unchallenged smile and a commendable empathy for the sorrowful living in squalor. Don Vinicio would laugh at the most inane happenings and when he got drunk there was nothing but cheer."

"Yes, you look extremely American, but I think your spirit lies somewhere else."

Soon enough we passed out of the city and into the countryside, out of the congested traffic and noise of downtown Riobamba. The sky opened up as the sun streaked down, its soft luminosity accentuating the green and brown of the rolling hills of the surrounding farmland. In the distance were great mountains: Chimborazo, Cotopaxi, Cayambe. We drove along cracked pavement at times shaky and uneven, taking quick turns around steep cliff sides, but my faith was entirely with Ana. Reckless and carefree, I had no qualms about putting my life entirely in her arms, which may not sound momentous by any means, but was of tremendous importance at the moment, since I had never felt that way about a girl before, or anyone for that matter.

As we pulled into the parking lot of the park I was sorry my camera had been stolen on the bus ride from the coast.

"Do you have a camera," I asked.

"Yes, in my purse on the floor."

I reached down and pulled a twenty dollar point-and-shoot camera from inside her purse. It wasn't digital, but I thought it quaint and only appropriate for such a spontaneous date. I loaded the film in the back and snapped the first photo of Ana in the driver's seat.

"Hey, you didn't say cheese!"

"Don't worry, you look beautiful just the way you are."

"Thank you, but I don't want to be remembered without a smile and I think you were looking down my blouse."

"Trust me, it was gold!" I remarked with a mischievous

31

grin.

The park was calm and abandoned except for a few wandering couples holding hands and families picnicking along the riverside. There was a wide expanse of green grassy fields, with llamas walking about alongside a wooden cabin set behind barbed wire fence. On either side were steep inclines of rock and bushes, a gentle stream trickling along the bottom of the hillside, a pond for paddling boats, and a fountain in the center decorated with concrete sculptures of saints and historical figures. We walked casually across the grass as Ana recounted the story of when she was a little girl and her father would take her here on Sunday afternoons following morning mass. We each snapped a few photos, posing on rocks or next to the llama, a creature which I found as passive as a bovine and more beautiful than a horse. There seemed to be some divine energy unfolding in this place, an eerie calm emanating from the gentle caress of the mountain winds gliding across the surface of the earth without pause or reflection.

Ana gently took my hand and led me across the field of grass, populated by small white flowers and swirling cypresses. We sat down by the river along an indentation in the ground that seemed perfect for resting one's head or making love if two people were so inclined. Holding her hand, glancing down at the calm and benevolent stream trickling along peacefully and occasionally exchanging glances, I was overwhelmed by the beauty of this place. Then as she caressed my palm and licked her lips I felt a sharp pang in my abdomen, as during my earlier occurrence of sexual arousal the night before.

"So, what do you think of my park?" she asked.

"It seems a bit," I managed to mutter as the pain grew deeper, "a bit; I'm not so sure, perhaps ordinary..."

"Ordinary? Isn't it beautiful?"

"Of course, of course, I meant extraordinary, it's breath-taking really. I mean..." I reached towards the pain and attempted to massage my stomach without seeming obvious or crude.

"Is something wrong?"

"No, not at all, please continue. I mean, what I'm trying to convey is that I'm overwhelmed by the sheer joy of being with you here, beneath this sun with the llamas and the river. Trust me; I think it's the most beautiful place I've ever seen."

"How long will you be here?"

"Till tomorrow at least."

"So, today is all we have?"

"It would seem that way. That is unless..."

"Unless what?"

"Unless something happens."

Then she leaned in toward me with a seductive gaze as I gently caressed her face and kissed her softly on the lips.

"Like that," she said.

"Yes, something like that," I replied, as my veins dilated, constricting the blood flow from my testes, causing them to swell and create a sharp and unforgiving pain in my abdomen. I jerked backward and grabbed my stomach, nearly shouting out in a chaotic rambling of every profanity I was aware of, as Ana looked on with astonishment and asked politely, "What's the matter?"

"Nothing really, just a stomachache I guess. I'm sorry to have ruined the moment, but I think I need some aspirin."

"Are you certain that's all you need? You look as though you're in a great deal of pain."

Words could not describe the immense shame I felt at this moment, realizing that Ana, the very object of my affection, was at least partially responsible for the pain in my abdomen, and yet if I revealed to her the source of my frustration, surely we would never have sex and I would die of embarrassment.

Attempting to deny my pain, I leaned in once again to resume our kiss, when she pulled back and said, "I think you need to see a doctor."

"No, really, I'll be alright. I must have just pulled a muscle or something, it's happened before."

"Are you sure, because the hospital isn't far."

"I'll be fine," I replied, "let's just enjoy the scenery and not worry so much about my testicl..."

"Your what?"

"Nothing, nothing, I mean perhaps we should be moving on."

"Alright," she consented, "there is more for you to see."

And just like that the moment was over and we headed back to the car without fulfillment of our kiss or our destiny. I knew I couldn't become amorously involved with this young woman for fear that my varicocele might act up in a horrific and ineffable pain that seemed unconcerned by my sincere wish to make love and be loved. As we drove out of the park and up along the hillside, Ana pointed out the pastures filled with bovines, the forests filled with swaying trees, and, although overcome with joy at being by her side in such an enchanting landscape, I could not escape the magnitude of the throbbing pain beneath my belt. Then, after some time, I realized I could not continue in the condition that I was in, and if I were in fact to have a sexual encounter with this girl this was not the time or place.

"About this hospital, how much would they charge?"

"That depends."

"Depends on what?"

"On the course of treatment."

"And what if it's nothing?"

"Then it will cost you nothing."

"You see, I've had this problem before and I'm not sure if

anyone here could fix it," I began to say as I realized I would have to divulge the secret. "It's not just a simple upset stomach; it's something a lot worse."

"And what would that be?"

"It's a varicocele, a swelling of the veins that drain the testes."

"You mean it's a problem with your *huevos*?"

"To put it bluntly, yes, it's a problem with my *huevos*."

She smiled, then began to laugh at the absurdity of the predicament. I felt ashamed, but could not deny the implicit humor in the situation and joined in with heartfelt laughter, which managed to ease the tension between us as she rubbed my arm and took hold of my palm, massaging it gently as a form of reassurance.

"Don't worry, I think the doctors will be able to fix your balls, we have good medicine here in Riobamba."

"Thank you for understanding, but I think I might need surgery."

"I don't think so, let's just wait and see."

"Drive quickly, I think it's getting worse, I don't know if I can manage this pain much longer, I only hope you're right."

Within fifteen minutes we were back in Riobamba, a drive that seemed much longer because of the immensity of my pain. I was glad it was out in the open despite the embarrassing nature of the situation, but at least I would have some medical attention and perhaps they could alleviate some of my suffering. As we entered the hospital, a modern concrete one-story complex, I saw many young children, some coughing , some with bandaged limbs, but none seemed to be in more urgent need of a doctor than myself, as by this time I could barely hobble my way in to see the nurse. A friendly young woman dressed in a white lab coat led me into a waiting room to be questioned concerning my symptoms. As my Spanish was hardly adequate for such purposes I had to keep Ana in the room as a translator.

"She wants to know what the problem is," related Ana.

"There's a pain in my abdomen and my left testicle is slightly enlarged, I think it has to do with a varicocele that I had treated eight years ago."

"How often does it hurt like this?"

"Occasionally, not often."

"When did it begin hurting this time?"

"Last night when I awoke from a dream."

"Is there anything that triggers it?"

"Yes."

"What?"

"I'd prefer not to say."

"I need to know, it may be important."

"Really! Is that necessary?"

"Yes!"

"Sexual arousal! Anything that might turn me on!"

"Oh, I see," remarked the nurse as I glanced over at Ana. "Well, I'll need to have a look."

Somewhat embarrassed by the nature of this ordeal I asked Ana to wait outside in the hallway. The nurse had me pull down my pants and examined my testicle. When she was finished she let Ana back in and related to her the situation.

"His testicle is slightly enlarged. I can recommend a urologist; he'll need to have an ultrasound to see if further attention is needed."

We both thanked the nurse and I hobbled back to the car with Ana to go see the specialist. We both refrained from speaking as we raced up and down the city with the urgency of impending doom, eventually arriving at the doctor's office as my pain grew with burning intensity, as if to say "not even in your dreams are you ever at peace."

We marched up some stairs to see the urologist, albeit in

painful contracted steps, and, surprisingly enough, were taken in to see the doctor after just a few short moments. Again my Spanish was not adequate to relate my condition, and Ana served as translator.

"So, what seems to be the problem?" he asked.

"I have a pain in my abdomen and an enlarged left testicle; I think it has to do with a varicocele I had treated eight years ago."

"You had surgery?"

"Yes, I had surgery eight years ago because of a similar problem. It went away for a while but reoccurs every so often."

"Did you recover?"

"Yes, I recovered for some years, but lately I've been having relapses during sexual situations."

He looked at Ana and asked, "Is this man your boyfriend?"

"No," she replied, "just a friend."

"I see, well, did this happen during intercourse?"

Ana looked at me with a jocular smile on her lips and we both began to laugh.

"No, no, no doctor, we were just sharing a kiss in the park when his balls began to act up. He's in excruciating pain. Is there anything you can do for him?"

"Well, to be sure about it we'll have to take an ultrasound of your testicles."

"Right now?"

"Yes, one of our nurses will take the ultrasound, and then we'll discuss a course of treatment."

They led me to another room while Ana waited out in the hallway. The nurse asked me to take off my pants and lie down on a thin metal table. I was surprised at how quick the whole process was between the hospital and getting an ultrasound of my swollen balls, considering it would take days back in the states and Ecuador isn't known for its quality of healthcare. The nurse rubbed gel on my scrotum, then gently massaged each testicle with a small pad as she snapped images that appeared on a screen as though I were having my first child. On the screen I could see her making marks along the images, labeling each testicle either *derecha* or *izquierda*. The left one was especially swollen, filled with some kind of oozing fluid. When the pictures were done she had me get dressed and I waited back out in the hallway with Ana.

"I'm sorry for kissing you," she remarked, "I didn't know you had a problem."

"I kissed you, remember? Besides, I don't really have a problem; this is just an unfortunate series of events set in place to remind me that while the world suffers so should I."

"That's certainly a bizarre way of looking at it."

"Even in heaven a man cannot be at peace."

"And this is your heaven?"

"No, this is the opposite of heaven. But, with you in the park it seemed pretty close."

Ana's eyes welled up as she looked me in the eyes and massaged my hand.

"That's so sweet. When this is through and we take care of your condition, we can go back if you'd like."

"I don't know, it might be too late, and I've got to get up early in the morning to make the bus to Banos."

"One more morning couldn't hurt; Macas isn't far."

"True."

Just then the doctor let us both into his office to admire my ultrasound.

"Look, it's our babies!" exclaimed Ana.

We both laughed and the doctor smiled, then proceeded with his diagnosis.

"You see the left testicle is swollen with fluid, creating

what is known as a hydrocele, which is often a complication that can follow surgery for a vericocele. You see this nodule at the bottom of the left testicle?" he asked as he pointed to the bottom of the chart. "This nodule is inflamed, leaking fluid into the sack that creates the swelling. Although relatively harmless, it can cause constrictions in the veins draining the testicles, which may be causing the pain in your abdomen. One option is minor surgery, which is safe, but can be relatively expensive. Other than that I can prescribe some medications that should alleviate the swelling and the pain in your lower abdomen."

"Can we get those filled here, doctor?" asked Ana.

"Some of them, but one is a bit complicated. Do you have any nursing experience?"

"Yes," she said, "my mother was a nurse."

"Well, it's up to you, but one of them needs to be carefully injected into his backside once every evening for the next five days."

"Really!" I exclaimed, "Is that really necessary?"

"Yes, if you want to recover as quickly as possible."

"I can take care of it doctor. He's under my watch."

"Well thank you, doctor, for your help," I said.

"Yes, thank you for your services, my friend, and I greatly appreciate it."

"Oh, and I would avoid sexual intercourse until the medicine is finished," said the doctor.

"Don't worry, we're just friends."

We left the urologist's office and headed down to the pharmacy, where we received twenty dollars worth of pills, vials of medicine, and a bunch of syringes that made me quiver.

"Are you sure you're up to it?"

"Trust me," she asserted, "I'm well-trained."

By the time we had left the office night had fallen over

Riobamba, and what had seemed so magical the night before, eternal sunshine radiating from every pore of the earth, slowly smoldered into the ashes of the mundane: busy streets filled with thousands of strangers speaking in foreign tongues, all-night fried chicken joints, cafes and bars that mocked me for my hydrocele and lack of proper walking habits. What could have been one of the most romantic days in my entire life morphed into the most extraordinarily painful one.

"We need bread and butter," declared Ana with enthusiasm.

"Bread and butter?" I inquired.

"Yes, but it must be fresh. I know just the place."

And just like that we were back in her car, skirting across the city in search of the most perfect loaf of bread and the most exquisite butter made fresh from local bovines. Ana drove like a madman up and down the city, obviously concerned for my condition as I was constantly moving up and down in my seat out of sheer frustration with both her driving and the immensity of my pain. We arrived back at my hotel to the dismay of the concierge.

This young hipster insisted that I wasn't allowed any visitors unless I paid for an extra bed.

"You don't understand," declared Ana, "I have to give him his medicine, an injection into his backside."

"I don't think so, no visitors allowed."

"Do you think we're trying to con you? Look! Look!" she exclaimed while holding up the syringes, "I'm his nurse and I must take care of him. It will only be a few minutes and then I'll leave."

The concierge looked incredulously at the two of us: one obviously an American on holiday, the other dressed in high black boots, skin tight jeans, and a tight-fitting blouse. I could imagine that he thought her to be a hooker, although she seemed way too classy to be a hooker, but he took note of the medicine and of the fact that I seemed to be in a great deal of pain. He looked us over and responded, "I'll give you ten minutes, but then she has to leave."

We both thanked him, rather vacuously, and then headed up to the third floor to my hotel room. We immediately lay down in bed, and Ana tore off pieces of bread, dipped them in butter and then fed them to me piece by piece.

"If only we had some wine," I remarked, "this might be very romantic."

"Don't you remember, I don't drink."

"Well, at least I could have some wine and you could perhaps have a glass of grape juice."

"Do you like this bread? It's the best in the city."

"It's delicious," I said, "the butter too."

"Well we don't have much time. Are you ready for your injection?"

"The question is: are you ready to inject me?"

"Turn over and pull down your pants, I'll take care of the rest."

"How romantic," I continued, "our first day together and you're already getting a good peek at my ass!"

I pulled down my pants and lay still on my stomach. Ana gently swabbed my left cheek and prepared the medicine.

"Be gentle," I said, "Don't force it."

"You'll only feel a slight prick; it's an old nurse's trick that my mother taught me growing up. Picture yourself back in the park, imagine the stream gently meandering down the hillside, and imagine the sky and the clouds. Feel the gentle caress of the wind gliding across your face. Can you picture it?"

"Yes, perfectly."

"Well, it's over, all through."

41

"Are you kidding me? Are you sure you got it all in?'

"Yes, I told you it wouldn't hurt. Now take your pills and try to get some sleep. I'll meet you outside by the stairs tomorrow morning at daybreak. There's some place I want you to see before you leave. Thank you for the beautiful afternoon. I'm glad we met."

"Where are you taking me tomorrow?"

"It's a secret; you'll just have to wait to find out."

"Thank you, Ana; I don't think anyone else in this world would be as sympathetic on a first date. To tell you the truth, I don't think there's much more we could go through in just twelve hours."

I pulled up my pants and sat on the edge of the bed. Ana gave me some pills and a glass of water, which I proceeded to swallow in the hope that tomorrow wouldn't be so awkward. Ana got up to leave, when I walked over for a hug.

"Goodnight Ana," I said as we embraced. Then I looked into her eyes and gently kissed her on the cheek. She drew back and paused, then kissed me deeply on the lips.

"Till tomorrow, my dear. Now get to bed."

Then, just as silently as she slipped into my life, she quietly abandoned me to my silent room. I disrobed, crawled beneath the sheets, and curled up in the corner of my bed. I wondered about the medicine, about my need for injections for the next four days, and about my plan to arrive in Macas in just three. Although disappointed that I would have to delay my excursion to the jungle, I felt thrilled that I would be forced to see Ana each and every night to receive my injection in the ass. If anything were to delay my work with ayahuasca, then certainly this was the best of possible outcomes, and who could foresee how the future would unfold. Perhaps if this harsh and unforgiving pain subsided there might be more in store than I had anticipated.

The night before I had felt alone, uncertain if I would see

Ana the following morning but thankful for the chain of events that had laid down the groundwork for our encounter. Tonight I was thankful again, not for a missed bus ride like before, but for the unreliable nature of my testicle. Yes, were it not for my swollen balls I might not be so fortunate. If a man's fate depends on the whim of events outside his control, is his fate merely an outcome of random coincidences? At this point I couldn't be sure either way, but I was equally glad of my fate and of the benevolence of whim.

I awoke early the next morning, just before sunrise and with my dreams at the forefront of my vision. Again, I was haunted by visions of the jungle; I had dreamt of a forgotten land in a foregone era. I had been immersed in the pulsing vibrations of a life-force more vibrant than mid-town Manhattan, but instead of being surrounded by electronic billboards I was enshrouded by the hum of insects and the loud screaming calls of birds and monkeys. I was alone, lost and forsaken it would seem, when a young child took my hand and led me down a dark and murky path. We emerged from the jungle into an encampment of Indians, a wide-open circle circumscribed by bamboo huts. At the center was a magnificent glowing fire, with men, women, and children gathered around sipping from shells. I was greeted by a towering holy man, with cheekbones cut from stone, a sharp crocodile tooth dangling from his neck. He greeted me in the language of his people, which I intuitively understood as "Welcome, young warrior of the light."

He grabbed me a piece of monkey flesh and a cup full *chicha*. I sat alongside the tribe on the outskirts of the fire as they chanted in a beautiful crescendo of voices singing soulfully in the night. They repeated again and again:

Yeah, he has returned
The lost son has emerged
From the depths of darkness
Our warrior of the light

He was lost but now is found
We sip on chica and devour
Our prey, the jungle is bountiful
And now we are safe

Our warrior of the light
Has returned from his trek
God is great, and now
We may sing once again

They continued to chant and sing, to drink, eat and be merry, like young children, honest and hopeful. The jungle hummed as well. I could sense the energy of the universe unfolding in this divine habitation of souls. They danced around the fire, and the children took me by the hand to dance as well. Late into the night we continued our celebration, and before I could awake a single phrase repeated itself, pounding on my eardrums:

Thank the heavens,
we are happy, we are thankful,
our warrior of the light
is back from his travels.

As I awoke from my dream, the haunting visions at the forefront of my brain receded silently into the night, drifting off into the obscurity along the jungle floor. My mind was lost in the canopies, as I crawled out of bed and into the shower. I couldn't help wonder what it all meant, why my mind kept retreating to a place and time that seemed so foreign. I was certain some deeper meaning was hidden amongst my nightly visions, urging me to move forward and continue my excursion to Macas to meet with Emiliano.

However, as the hot water poured down my naked body, I was reminded of my date with Ana and was thankful I would be by her side for the next four days. The jungle beckoned from the horizon, but with a terrifying visage. What I was to encounter at the edge of civilization my mind could only ponder. As I stepped out of the shower and dressed for the day's events, the sun peeked through the window shade and a soft luminosity gently painted the room with a pinkish hue, like the color of a young rose finally emerging from its bud. I checked the clock and quickly prepared to head downstairs. I grabbed a knapsack and headed out the door, thankful that the pain in my abdomen had subsided and I could walk free of worries concerning my hydrocele.

Down in the lobby Ana was waiting on a bench. She stood up, gave me a hug and observed, "I see you can walk again. The medicine must be working."

"I suppose, for the moment; let's wait and see what the day has in store for us."

Then she continued, "I think you should gather your stuff and move to another hotel. I can find you one much cheaper, closer to the center of the city."

"Are you sure?" I asked.

"Trust me; there are more agreeable establishments in this town."

I ran upstairs and cleared out my things, paid my bill and departed for the day's events.

"So, where are we heading so early in the morning?" I asked.

"We're heading to Guano, a small town on the outskirts of Riobamba; there's a hot spring up in the mountains. It's empty in the early morning and we should have the place to ourselves," she said as she drove nervously out of the city.

Unlike yesterday afternoon the streets were empty. We passed through Riobamba and out into the hillsides. Off in the distance, the sun was rising above the horizon, the morning air was chill but the soft rays of sunlight warmed my skin. The road grew steeper as we ascended into the mountains, large empty plots of farmland along one side and a precipitous slope on the other. Some short, dark-skinned Indian men and women were tending their fields as we slowly crept up the hillside.

At one point Ana slowed down and asked an elderly gentleman the way to the springs. He pointed us to the left, and in a matter of minutes we had reached our destination. The parking lot was empty; it seemed we were the first to arrive. Past the entrance gates, beyond some changing rooms, set back against mountainside along a swift running stream were two small pools of steaming water. We slipped silently into one of the pools, which felt scalding at first, but a welcome change from the frigid morning air. We floated around for a minute or two, neither of us saying a word, by ourselves up in the mountains enjoying the comfort of the volcanic heat underneath our warm bath of water.

"So are you going to leave me after this?" asked Ana, finally breaking the silence.

"How could I, you're my nurse."

"So, you're going to stay till Saturday?"

"Looks that way, until the medicine is finished."

"Are you still in any pain?"

"Not much, nothing too intense, nothing like yesterday."

"Then the medicine is a success!"

"Let's not be hasty."

"Are you still intent on your trip to the jungle?"

"Of course."

"And what will you do there?"

"I've arranged to work with a shaman, with the indigenous medicine ayahuasca."

"And why are you interested in ayahuasca?"

"Can't a man be curious?"

"Can't a woman be curious about the curiosity of a man? Especially a young American man interested in uncovering his secret fate with a powerful and exotic drug."

"It's not a drug!" I exclaimed.

"What else but a drug would so distort the senses and contort the body into compulsive spasms of vomiting and excreting? What else but a drug would make a man feel as though he is flying above the earth? What else but a drug would make a man feel as though he's communicating with alien life forms? What else I ask you?"

"So, have you tried it?"

"No, of course not!"

"Aren't you curious about my curiosity?"

"You Americans are so damn intrigued by the exotic. If you could buy ayahuasca in a supermarket, and they told you that it might trigger vomiting and diarrhea, you wouldn't be nearly so damn curious! But an Indian goes off into the forest and collects some foliage, then prepares an insidious tea from composted jungle, and you travel half way around the world just to get a sip."

"It's more than a tea," I continued, "it's a conduit be-tween realities, between the waking and the unwaking, between the living and the inert, between the world of the here and now and the one beyond. I've only tried it once, but it's the most beautiful thing I've ever seen, grander than any mountainside, more elegant than the petal of any flower. It's a highly-evolved intelligence that provides access to the spiritual world for the duration of an evening. How, I ask, could a man pass that up?"

"Let's not talk about it right now, no point in spoiling the time we have with each other. This pool is too hot. Would you like to rinse off in the river?"

"I don't know, it looks icy cold."

"That's because it is icy cold! Now let's take a dip."

We emerged from the super-heated pool and plunged into the river. We washed ourselves below a small waterfall in the frozen clutch of the small mountain stream, which invigorated my spirit and awoke me to the reality of the event. I took it for granted that Ana and I were here together in Guano after just having met this past Monday and this was perhaps my greatest adventure yet. Fully awake and conscious of the inevitable fact that nothing lasts for more than a fleeting moment, I grasped Ana and kissed her on the lips.

"Let's get out of here," she said, and we dissolved our-selves, our hearts, our bodies and minds, back into the springs.

"Will I see you again?" I asked.

"What do you mean?"

"I mean after I leave, will we ever see each other again, or is this just a dream?"

"I don't believe in dreams, because when you awake they always wash away."

"How could you not believe in dreams? They're the life-force of all creation, they stem from the unconscious will of the collective human psyche, they allow us to believe in something grander than ourselves. If we abandon our dreams we abandon our destiny."

"Destiny is intuitive, we follow our own paths accord-ingly, but dreams are of a different earth. Perhaps we could call them unearthly. We mustn't necessarily listen to our dreams, but rather heed our intuition."

"And what does your intuition tell you?" I asked.

"I don't know, that's hard to say, I don't know where I'm heading, maybe to Holland or maybe to Spain, but there's always the hope I suppose, nothing's impossible."

"Why would you head to Spain?"

"To see my sister and my niece, they live in Spain and I haven't seen them in over four years."

"Maybe I could meet you in Spain, I've always wanted to hike El Camino de Santiago, and perhaps you could join me on my pilgrimage."

"You are a pilgrim, aren't you? Are you seeking salvation?"

"In a way, I suppose."

"And why should you be saved? What evil have you done?"

"Not sure, but I'm haunted by demons. The doctors told me I have a mental illness, but I don't trust doctors or diagnoses. I was thinking perhaps this shaman might have some answers, might reveal to me the root of my mental anguish. I've been having strange dreams of the jungle, a place I've never been to and have only seen on television and in movies. They call me the warrior of the light, they sing so soulfully in celebration of my return. Why would a people in a faraway land welcome a stranger and embrace him as their own?"

"Dreams are dreams; they have no meaning but the one you give them. They stem from the unconscious. We all have absurd visions as we lay our heads to sleep, but they're not necessarily useful in predicting the future or guiding our everyday actions. Perhaps your dreams are deluding you, or perhaps you have delusions that invoke dreams of the jungle--but don't seek salvation in the unearthly realm of the unconscious. If you're seeking to understand your mind then look no further than the present."

"How do you mean?"

"Absolution can only be found in realizing the present moment. The past is a dream, and the future is uncertain, the only consolation can be found in the now. What are you thinking now? What do you feel now? Is there anything more absurd than thinking there is more to life than the present?"

Intuitively, I understood what Ana was saying. I had experienced the tremendous power of the present moment the day before at the café, staring at my coffee and reveling in the awesome wonder and awe of my cream stirring up galaxies and, in a matter of seconds, imploding stars. I couldn't abandon the feeling that my dreams were of tremendous importance, but it seemed silly to dwell on the insubstantial material of an ethereal nature. What mattered was the mere fact that I had Ana by my side, basking in the morning light amongst the majestic poetry of the surrounding landscape. I was warm, I was secure, I was happy and content, and what mattered more than anything, I was in the company of a good friend who would not leave me if I chose to remain present.

"I'm glad we're here," I told Ana.

"So am I," she said as she put her arms around me and held me tightly. We sat like that for some time, enjoying the peace and quiet, the warm water and the beautiful countryside. Soon enough other people showed up at the springs, an elderly man or two, a family now and then, until the place was humming with activity and our silence became a familiar gathering, a public setting in which to dissolve the passing quiet of our moment in time. As the early morning headed toward noon we dried ourselves off, changed clothing, and then headed back to the car and down the mountainside.

Nearly a moment or two after leaving I felt a longing for that place, an intense sentimental attachment that would only grow with time and eventually burden me with nostalgia for the past, but for now we were on to our next adventure. Ana drove us to a small town just a few miles outside of Riobamba. We parked the car and walked the streets, ducking in and out of some local shops displaying artisan handicrafts. The sun was now approaching its zenith as the air grew warm and the intensity of the sun's rays became burdensome.

We stopped at a café serving soup, meat and potatoes for lunch. Ana ordered our meals in the polite and benevolent manner with which she treated everyone, as though they were close friends, which could have been the case for all I knew, and which I was slowly becoming accustomed to. She displayed an unchallenged and commendable cheer for life and its people in her actions and in her mannerisms; she seemed to me at that moment and in every moment since our encounter one of the most attractive human beings I had ever had the pleasure to know. I couldn't help wondering why she wasn't married with children, or at least in a relationship, which begged the question: "Do you have a boyfriend or husband I'm not aware of?"

She laughed at the remark, possibly finding it inane or incidental, as though to brush it aside, then replied, "Do you think I would kiss you or let you kiss me if I were involved?"

"No," I replied, "you seem too honest to allow something like that, but I can't figure you out, you're so perfect in every way that it seems unfathomable that you could be alone."

"Are you a religious man, Jack?"

"I try to be."

"Then you probably already know that we are never truly alone, and even if you don't believe in God or a higher power you must have realized by now that the world is filled with lonely people whether they are attached or not. I've been in relationships and still felt lonely, but I think the key to life is to fulfill yourself before you can fill anyone else. A good partnership can only be forged once both parties have found themselves and completed themselves. Then they may begin to try and complete each other. Call it God, call it the life force of all creation, but once we fill ourselves with divine love and compassion, then and only then may we seek the companionship of a fellow human being."

"So, you're a saint, aren't you?"

"We should all be saints."

"Well, at least answer this: have you ever been in love? You couldn't have always been a saint; you must have fallen head over heels in love at some point or another."

"How' bout you?"

"Me? No, never."

"Honestly?

"I'm afraid; it scares the living shit out of me!"

"So, you've never fallen for someone?"

"I've come close."

"But never all the way?"

"I can't afford to submit to that kind of pain. I would never heal, I would never recover once I lost what I had found."

"Yeah, it would be too much pain, right?" she said with a sly trace of sarcasm.

"Exactly."

"Kind of like yesterday, right?"

"That was an entirely different sort of pain, that's a pain that heals."

"But you've felt it before, with a woman, I would suppose?"

"That's just sex! Sex is recreation, love is dangerous."

"So, you believe in sex without love?" she asked.

"I don't know what I believe in, but if you're asking if I've had sex without being in love, then the answer is yes."

"Well, perhaps this is just the saint in me, but I believe that sex is more than recreation, it's an act of commitment, the shared trust and partnership of two people in love with each other."

"You are a saint, aren't you?"

"Are you Catholic?"

"I try to be."

"Then you should try harder," she said as the waitress

came with our meals. Ana thanked her politely as she retreated to the back of the café where her family was busy eating lunch and watching television. We sat in silence for a moment or two, eating our meat and potatoes beneath the humming electricity of an afternoon cartoon.

"I'm sorry," started Ana, "I don't mean to judge you; I suppose I let my morals get the better of me sometimes."

"Hey, if you didn't have your morals, who would you be?"

"Like you, I suppose."

"Hey, I have morals, but I'm still human. I make mistakes and then regret the mistakes I've made, but as far as I can tell morals are only guidelines and shouldn't be adhered to in any kind of bureaucratic fashion. We need to be human, to hope for the best, but plan for the worst. Ideals are well and good for the mind, but action requires more than thought. You've got to expect things to go astray, then cope as best you can. I admire your idealism, but life is a messy affair and if you don't get a little dirty now and again then perhaps you never really lived."

"A little dirt never hurt anyone," she replied, "but ideals aren't meant to keep us clean. No one ever said that moral sentiments were going to provide salvation for the soul. That can only come through sincere faith and penitence for one's sins. No, morality provides the best possible outcome for all situations because even when you get a little dirty, you know deep down that you acted in accord with your beliefs. You said you're afraid of attachment because you're afraid of loss, but I think what you don't realize is that life itself is a form of loss. Conception doesn't only mean birth, because birth itself means death. So, if you're afraid of death then why live at all? Why do anything, because one day it's all going to be taken away?"

"I didn't say that at all. I'm not afraid of death or afraid to live, I'm afraid of the emotional pain that comes with loss. The less you attach yourself to the world, the less chance of suffering. I've already suffered enough and I can't bear the thought of suffering more."

"But death is the greatest loss of all. If you're not afraid to die, then you are finally free to face the sufferings of life."

"But aren't those sufferings the true loss?"

"No, the true loss is when they are finally all taken away. I don't think you have an illness, but perhaps you are still afraid."

"To form attachments?"

"Or maybe to let them go."

A silence ensued our escalating conversation. We paused, gathered our wits and finished our meals. Outside storm clouds were gathering in the east and soon thick pellets of rain were showering down. We ran to the car to take refuge. Ana looked over and announced her plans.

"I'm going to take you to a new hotel in the center of the city near the train station. I have some things to attend to, but I'll be back tonight to give you your medicine. Sound ok?

"Sounds ok."

"You won't be lonely?"

"The world is a lonely place."

Silence ensued between us as we drove out of the countryside back into the chaotic mess of traffic that consumes Riobamba around that time of day. Ana parked the car illegally along a busy section of the city as we ran into the hotel to arrange for a new room. Ana spoke with the owner in the barely coherent Spanish that I was not accustomed to, then turned to me and said, "It's going to be about five bucks a night. He said visitors aren't allowed in the evening, but I've arranged some time to give you your medicine later on when I return. Sound reasonable?"

"You mean we can't hang out?"

"Just for a few minutes while I give you your medicine."

"That's too bad; I was hoping you could stay the night."

She smiled at me with a foolish grin, and then said, "Don't get ahead of yourself."

"Well, don't be long with the chickens, I may get bored."

"I have to visit with my mom; she's concerned about my mysterious disappearance this morning. I told her I was visiting friends, but I think she's worried."

"That wasn't very saintly of you."

"Well, most saints don't have a mother like mine."

"Tell her your friends kept you in good company, and send our regards."

"I'll be back soon, shouldn't be long. Get some food and enjoy the city, there's plenty for you to see."

"Don't worry," I said, "I'll be fine."

Then she gave me a hug, smiled brightly and headed out the door.

I greeted the amiable woman behind the desk as she gave me the key to my room and provided some towels.

"You have a lovely friend," she said in Spanish.

"Thank you," I acknowledged, "she's precious." Then I headed through the lobby, past a guest watching daytime novellas, around a corner to room number seven. The room was rather large for five bucks a night, with high ceilings, a private bathroom with warm running water and my own television set. I set down my things, unpacked my clothing, rinsed off in the shower, and then prepared to head out for dinner. As I did so I was suddenly reminded that I hadn't spoken with my mother in over a week. Last we spoke I had plans of heading down to Peru to see Machu Pichu and hike the Inca Trail. Little did my parents know of the serendipitous unfolding of the past few days' events, and although I thought it only appropriate to give them a call and announce my plans to see the jungle, I figured some things were best left unsaid. With that in mind I left the hotel and headed out into the busy center of city to find a decent payphone with reasonable rates. Night was fast approaching and as the dark descended on Riobamba, I felt ambivalence about my own situation. Not that I was unsure about my course of action. I certainly wanted to spend as much time with Ana as possible. Still healing from the other day, I was sure I needed medicine, but the jungle was calling out from the back of my mind, and I felt an urgency to depart as soon as possible.

I entered a phone booth boasting calls to the U.S. for under twenty cents a minute, dialed my number and waiting in silence as I listened to the ring tone.

"Hello," answered a familiar voice, gentle and inviting.

"Mom, it's me, Jack!"

"Jack, where are you?" she exclaimed with a sense of urgency.

"I'm still in Ecuador, a large city, Riobamba, up in the highlands."

"Oh! Jack, I'm so glad you didn't head to Lima. There's been a terrible earthquake, the city's in shambles, hundreds killed. Oh, I'm so glad! We haven't heard from you since you were on the coast and thought you might have left already."

"Seriously? Hundreds killed?"

"Well, maybe not hundreds, but it's chaos down there. Where are you heading?"

"I'm on my way to the Amazon, to a jungle town called Macas to meet with some friends. What a fortunate series of events!"

"What do you mean?"

"I'll tell you all about it when I get home."

"Oh, I'm just thankful you're not down in Peru right now, I hope you're still enjoying your trip. Be careful in the jungle, I hope you're not venturing into the Amazon alone. Isn't that dangerous?"

"Yes, very. I've arranged to stay with some folks in Macas for a week. Should be departing out of Quito the Wednesday after. Hope all is well back in Jersey, but I've got to go now, these calls aren't cheap. Send my love to Dad and Dylan. I'll be in touch before I leave."

"Be careful, honey. Have fun and I'll hear from you later in the week."

"Bye bye!"

"Goodbye!"

A sense of relief washed across my body as I hung up the phone, and my ambivalence solidified into a sense of fate. Not that it was so strange that I would opt to stay in Ecuador and not pursue Peru, but it felt strangely fortunate that I was here in Riobamba, when for all the world cared, I could be stuck beneath the rubble of a city in distress hundreds of miles to the south. Had I departed Guayaquil for Lima I would have arrived just prior to the earthquake, and now because of a path I was following out of pure intuition under the guidance of dreams, I was safe and sound in Ecuador in the care and company of a lovely woman whom I had just encountered two nights earlier.

As I stepped outside a thunderstorm was brewing, I could hear cracks of thunder as the sky opened up and the rain came flooding down. I quickly made my way along the dark streets filled with restaurants, internet cafes, and local shops selling everything from electronics to sweaters made from llama fiber. I passed one store selling jewelry and ducked in out of the rain to take a look. The shopkeeper greeted me warmly and asked if I needed any help.

"I'm looking for something for my girlfriend," I said.

"Well, I have plenty of fine jewelry to choose from," she said. "What does she like?"

"I'm looking for something simple," I replied, "maybe

just a bracelet."

"Do you love her?" she asked.

"Of course I love her."

"Well, then how about this?" she replied as she motioned to a necklace with a silver heart-shaped locket.

I opened it up and inside were inscribed the words *"Te Amo Por Siempre."*

"How much?" I asked

"Ten dollars."

"Ten dollars! I'll give you five."

"Eight."

"Six."

"All right, I'll give it to you for seven dollars."

"Thank you."

She put the necklace in a small pouch then wrapped it up and took my money. "Good luck, I hope things work out."

"Goodnight!"

Outside the stormwater was flooding down avenues, forming small rivers nearly impossible to avoid. I was navigating my way along the puddles and streams, frantically searching for a decent restaurant, when I spotted a pizza place across the intersection. Although drenched to the bone and in dire need of a dry place to rest, I was very fond of thunderstorms and found the entire ordeal a welcome respite from the afternoon heat. I crossed the street and entered the restaurant, quickly removed my rain jacket and attempted to dry off. Behind the counter was a large brick oven, and a friendly gentleman who lead me to a comfortable spot beside the window on the edge of the dining area. The place was crowded with people, some locals, some who looked foreign. I sat down by myself and tried to relax, and although I've become accustomed to dining alone, I couldn't expect to find doing so all that enjoyable. This must have been one of those touristy joints, as I could see they offered an unusually large variety of pizzas, a food which I think the Ecuadorians have never quite taken seriously because they always forget the most vital ingredient: the tomato sauce.

When my waiter returned I ordered the Hawaiian and attempted in my poor and possibly offensive Spanish to describe tomato sauce.

"Can you put the sauce of tomato on it?" I asked.

"*Salsa de tomate*?" he inquired.

"*Sí*," I replied.

I sat quietly, enjoying the loud rap of rain against the windowsill, admiring the city that was fast becoming a swimming pool, and contemplated the days ahead. I was becoming very fond of Ana, and I sensed that she was becoming very fond of me. Although my original intent when I went scouring the city Monday evening for an attractive woman was to get laid and move on to the next city, I found that my dubious intentions had become compromised when I discovered that beauty, intelligence, sincerity, and humility are not always mutually exclusive qualities in a woman and occasionally a woman that possesses these qualities is not only single, but within my reach. Although our first day together was one of the most painful and embarrassing ordeals of my entire life, I found it funny and surprisingly appropriate that my testicle problem prevented this sincere, mature, and utterly amazing woman from slipping through my fingers. After giving it some thought I decided that I would do everything in my power not to let this girl get away. I realized this was her home and her mother and sister, friends and acquaintances might find it absurd and possibly dangerous for her to be hooking up with some American backpacker dude, but it had become my new intention--my fantastically moral and upright intention--to form a relationship.

As these thoughts filtered through my head and my

resolve grew firm I noticed some European backpackers motioning toward my table.

"Come sit with us," they said, "you look lonely."

"Sure," I responded, then picked up my things and moved over to their table.

"Where are you from?" asked the woman in an obviously German accent; she was dressed from head to toe in breathable, water resistant, polyester North Face apparel.

"New Jersey."

"The States?"

"Yep, so you guys are from Germany?"

"No, we're from Holland," said the man, a thirty-something guy with a round face, short brown hair, and a blossoming beard.

"Oh really, my friend is trying to get a position with the Embassy in Holland, but she doesn't speak Dutch."

"Where's your friend from?

"She's from Riobamba, I met her two days ago."

"Well, does she speak English?"

"Flawlessly."

"Then she may have a shot."

"Where are you coming from?" asked the woman with a friendly looking face, soft features, delicate eyes, and short brown hair.

"I was living on the coast for a while in a small village about fifteen minutes south of Puerto Lopez."

"Really!" she exclaimed. "We're on our way to Montanita, not far from there."

"And where are you coming from?"

"Well, we started six months ago in Brazil, wound our way down to Argentina and Chile, then up through Bolivia and into Peru."

"True backpackers! I'm extremely jealous, I'll be leaving in two weeks, but I wish I had more time. There's so much to see in just one country."

"There's even more to see in just one continent."

"Did you get to the Amazon?"

"Yes, in both Bolivia and Peru. We took a two-week trip down in Peru just before we headed up to Ecuador. Very beautiful, one of the most amazing experiences of the entire trip! You must see it for yourself, it's indescribable."

"Really? I'm heading to Macas in a few days, not for the wildlife but to work with a shaman of the Shuar tribe."

"How exciting!" exclaimed the man. "Will you be working with ayahuasca?"

"Have you tried it?"

"Yes, once, with ambiguous results."

"How do you mean?'

"Well, I'm not certain if you're aware, but ayahuasca tastes like pure shit!"

"Yes, I'm aware."

"Like month-old jungle compost had been pureed in a blender and then served like a hot fresh steaming piece of dog shit!"

I laughed.

"So, as you're aware, I had some trouble keeping it down. I vomited a little too early and I don't think the drug got into my system fully. No real visions, just more vomiting and shitting, couldn't keep anything in me, must have lost ten pounds in a matter of hours. I remember lying there in total heaving, vomiting, shitting sickness thinking a conman shaman had poisoned me, while the real stuff was hidden in the bush."

"No, that sounds like the medicine alright. It's a dizzying, blurry sickness, but if you get it down good and it's the right stuff the ride will take your breath away."

"So, you've experienced it?'

"Once. It was painful and joyous wrapped in more sickness and a dizzying array of complex and utterly fantastic, otherworldly visions. I had a taste, then woke up and decided I'd travel half way across the country to throw down five hundred bucks to puke and shit my guts out for seven days."

"Seven days?!"

"Yep, I'll be working with Emiliano Tséremp, the renowned shaman of the Shuar tribe. Been working with the stuff for forty-odd years, supposed to be a real professional."

"Where'd you meet him?"

"Haven't met him yet; we were introduced through the wife of a drug dealer I met in Montanita by the name of Rodrigo. If you're looking for another shot, or looking to score some coke he's a wild-haired Colombian with lots of tattoos and a demeanor of recklessness and 'I don't give a shit.'"

"And this is your friend?"

"I'm intrigued by the wild ones."

"Well, we'll make sure not to find him," added the woman.

I laughed.

"It's hard not to, he's everywhere at once. By the way, if you're not looking to surf or party really fucking hard you might want to avoid Montanita, it's a tourist trap anyway."

"Thanks for the advice; we'll see when we get there."

Just then our pizzas arrived and I looked down and noticed my Hawaiian covered in ketchup.

"What's *salsa de tomate*?" I asked the woman.

"You got it alright."

"Fuck! I tell you, I think the recipe for pizza got lost in translation on the way down from the States. I ask for *salsa de tomate* and they give me a ketchup-covered cheese bread!"

They smiled and laughed, the man nearly spitting up his drink.

"Maybe the sauce is too expensive."

"Or maybe my Spanish is just plain inadequate."

We dove into our meals, spoke a bit more about our travels, and then I politely excused myself to get back to the hotel in time to meet Ana. The rain was still falling, so I nearly had to swim back to the hotel, just hoping Ana wouldn't get held up with her mom and the hundreds of hungry chickens.

To my welcome surprise she was waiting patiently in the lobby with a brown paper bag. She gave the lady behind the desk a friendly nod, then we headed back to room number seven.

"You're soaked," she announced.

"I didn't have a car that I could park illegally."

"Well, are you ready for the medicine?"

"Wow, you're all business tonight."

"We only have a few minutes, so let's get this over with."

I politely laid on the bed face down, then gently pulled down my pants.

"No need for the bedtime story about the clouds and the park, just give it to me straight."

"Alright, if you insist," she said as she prepared the medicine and poked it in without restraint.

"Ow! I kind of liked that in a bizarre and sick perverted kind of way. Do you have to leave me so soon?"

"Yes, but I have a surprise bit of information for you."

"What?"

"Well, I was thinking about our predicament and my mother is getting a bit suspicious, so I told her I was going to take a trip with some friends to Banos for a few days so we could share some time before your trip to Macas."

A pause.

"That's the most ingenious plot such a saint could ever devise, perhaps only a saint could devise. "I love you!" I blurted out.

Ana smiled nicely and her eyes lit up with joy. "I'll meet you in the lobby tomorrow morning at ten o'clock, so get up early, pack up your stuff and get some breakfast before I arrive."

Then she got up to depart and gave me a gentle caress along my forehead and a soft kiss on the lips.

"Sleep tight, my dear, dream sweet dreams, and I'll see you in the morning."

And like that, she slipped silently out the door as I sat in bed with my pants still down. I took out the pouch with the locket and peeked inside.

"*Te Amo por siempre*, my dear," I said softly beneath my breath as I pulled the sheets over my head and prepared for the visitation of unearthly, beautiful, exotic and enchanting vistas to overwhelm my senses and transport me across space and time only to end up back where I started to hold the most dear and precious thing I had ever found, hoping, NO! praying that when I awoke, if really I had indeed ever awakened in the first place, that this wasn't some fantastic, demented, insane plot invented by the novelty of my own ego-seeking, utterly insane imagination to deceive my senses with the ruse that this was not just a dream. I held tight to the locket and whispered again and again beneath my breath, "*Te Amo por Siempre, Te Amo por Siempre*," until the internal lights faded and all was dark and silent, splendid and joyous, lovely and perfect.

Dark and silent, blank and quiet. I awoke in the early morning with a nervous excitement trembling from my toes to my fingertips. My dreams from last night were still at the forefront of my vision, dissolving quickly in the haze of light streaming in through the window shades. As before, I was visited by a fearsome shaman of ancient lore cleansing me with ceremonial banana leaves so as to purify my spirit before it ascended to the ethereal plane of unearthly vistas.

From a large hand-rolled cigar he blew smoke up and down my body, while waving palm fronds.

"Are you ready?" He asked.

"I think so," I replied.

"No, you are not ready," he responded with a firm hand. "The medicine can only heal those that are ready to be healed. You must let go before you can begin."

"Begin what?" I asked

"Begin healing your body and mind. Only then may the spirit ascend."

"I think I'm ready," I repeated.

"No, you are not ready. Only when you've given up on this world may you enter the next."

A pause. I felt frustrated, confused and anxious. How can I give up when I don't even know what it is I'm giving up? I felt a heavy weight pushing me down, the burden of existence weighing on me more heavily then I could ever recall. I felt sick with this burden, with this heaviness. I wanted to purge, to vomit and excrete my entire being to the point of existing as nothing but pure, exalted energy. I tired of the material realm and desired the next, a desire that was destroying me because of its impossibility. How could I give up something that could not be given up? How could I purge myself of something that could not be purged?

"I'm ready for the medicine," I repeated. "I'm ready to give up."

"No, you are not ready," he said once more. "Desire is a thing of the past, body and mind are things of the past, everything you know and love is a thing of the past. The spirit may only ascend when you have finally given up."

Confused and irritated, disoriented and disappointed, I felt ashamed of my incompetence, ashamed of my attachment to the physical realm that I never knew existed. The weight was now overbearing, pushing on me from all sides, pressing on my temples. This weight was destroying me, tearing me to shreds from the sheer pressure of its boundless force. Then, just as escape seemed impossible, so far from my grasp that my surrender seemed imminent, I recognized something that seemed out of place. A silly grin spread across my face, and I chuckled with ecstatic glee as I heard a voice from the farthest recesses of my consciousness.

"Let it destroy you," commanded the voice, "let it all come crashing down."

"What?" I asked.

"Give up!"

Unable to hold off the sheer burden of this unfathomable force any longer, I listened to the silly little voice from deep within; I accepted my fate and submitted to its will. Just then, just as I was ready to awaken, the burden was released and I fell into a bottomless void as a vortex of energy consumed my senses, my mind and body--my entire existence as I was aware of it--only to spit me out the other side as a pure streak of light. The weight released as the force consumed itself, feasted on its own entrails until all that existed was nothingness, empty space without form or being.

"I'm ready," I repeated, "Now, I am ready."

"Yes, you are ready," the shaman answered, "now you are ready."

Breath entered my body as I awoke from my dream, both startled and filled with untarnished joy. The silly grin would not subside as I climbed out of bed and prepared for the day's events. Wonder and awe of the external world entered my mind as I was still caught in the throes of my epic struggle with the burden of existence. I was overcome with the beauty of the most trivial details of my room: the flower-printed patterns on the bedspread, the soft streaks of light filtering through the windowsill, the hum of voices whispering from the television set out in the lobby. Everything emanated beauty and joy, a calm, reflective peace that could not be destroyed.

I prepared for the day and then headed across the street to get some breakfast. The torrential downpour had subsided, and the sun came out, glancing down on the world with soft streaks of light. I unbuttoned my jacket and sat down at a local café. While waiting for my coffee I recalled Ana's suggestion from the night before. Surely there could not be a more perfect turn of events; we were both on our way to Banos, if only to part on my way down to Puyo. By this time the sharp and unforgiving pain in my abdomen had relinquished its grasp and subsided to a dull and practically unrecognizable discomfort. And with my hydrocele in check there was no telling what fortune awaited us on our trip to Banos. I began to consider this our honeymoon, not so much an introduction to a lifetime of matrimony, but a lifetime of loneliness upon our departure. This fact weighed on me as my waitress brought my coffee and eggs. I had come to the firm conclusion the night before to make every effort within my capability to make this work.

Back at the hotel Ana was waiting for me in the lobby, looking rather casual in a white and pink sweat suit getup.

"Are you ready, my love?" she asked.

"As ready as can be, I suppose."

She stood up and gave me a hug, "Let's get your bag and be on our way."

We cleared out my room and drove to the bus station. I noticed in her expression and demeanor a clear reflection of my own nervous excitement, her slender, refined fingers trembling on the steering wheel, her subtle smile glowing pure radiance. I felt calm in her presence, but not subdued by the tedious boredom that comes with familiarity. I felt I had known her forever, but with a novelty that could only be explained by the unusual circumstances of our encounter. What madness is this strange tide of fate, what explanation could account for two particles, so far and so distant, floating on a sea of doubt and confusion, find one another and latch on for the better? Our union, as it was, might be an impermanent one, just as all things living must one day pass on, but our cores were inextricably bound, molded and shaped by the character of our actions, and the language of our tongues. I wasn't prepared to unleash these ponderous thoughts on Ana, but I could sense in her eyes, in the gesture of her lips that I wasn't merely a passing acquaintance and that her intentions were just as moral and upright as my ideals.

"What's the matter?" she asked, noting my reflective demeanor.

"I was just thinking how sad it is that this medicine is working so quickly."

"So, your balls are healing?"

"My balls are well."

"Then you should be glad."

"I am, I just wish we had more time."

"Time is precious, we must cherish the time we have."

A pause.

"Are we so crazy?"

"Crazy for what?"

"Are you crazy for trusting me? And am I crazy for

leaving you?"

"But you haven't left me yet."

"But I will."

"And why shouldn't I trust you, don't you trust me?"

"With every ounce."

"And I the same."

"I'm already regretting leaving you."

"Then don't leave."

"I'll come back."

"I trust you will."

She parked the car just outside the bus terminal and we hauled my backpack to the ten o'clock leaving for Banos. We bought our tickets and boarded, settling down in a comfortable seat somewhere near the back. She sat by the window and I looked out toward the market, dozens of men and women selling fruit and clothing, trinkets and DVDs, leather wallets and belts, shoes and sandals, flowers and herbs. I admired the vendors for their diligence and work ethic; I admired them for the simplicity of their actions and the art of their craftsmanship. Part of me longed to be one of them, to worry about worldly matters, to put food on the table and enjoy the company of good friends and family. I wanted a simple life, like that of a child, to have faith in God and trust his path is holy and righteous. As our bus began to part Ana made the sign of the cross on her chest, forehead and shoulders and offered a prayer to a higher power to guide us on our journey and bring us safely to our destination. I watched her with some hesitation, then did the same and prayed for the both of us.

We departed Riobamba amongst the early morning traffic; headed out into the hills with mountains towering in the distance. I put my arm around Ana and we enjoyed the sights of the passing scenery. Occasionally the bus stopped and let people on: men, women and children of all shapes and sizes, skin colors and ethnic origins. Young children sold oranges, popsicles, and plastic containers holding rice and chicken. We bought some bread and enjoyed each other's company. The bus took sharp turns around precipitous slopes, thousand foot ravines descending into tumultuous rivers. We looked down in awe and Ana held me tight.

"Are you frightened?" I asked.

"Yes," she nodded.

"Have faith," I replied, "What's meant to be is meant to be."

"Do you mean that if we were meant to die then we will die?"

"It's out of our hands."

"I have faith," she replied.

"Faith is enough," I responded.

A nod.

"Can I ask you a question?"

"Yes, what is it?"

"What did you think of me when we first met?"

"Honestly?"

"Of course."

"I thought that you had a silly hat, but that you were cute."

"Did you ever imagine that we would end up like this?"

"Not then."

"What were you doing at the café so late at night?"

"I was bored."

"Do you find your life boring?"

"Sometimes. My mother and I had been arguing bitterly over the family business and I needed some time to think."

"And so that's what brought you to me?"

"I suppose. I was about to leave when you entered, but I thought you were handsome and I noticed you look in my direction with a smile."

"Honestly?"

"Yes, there was a childlike innocence in your demeanor and I could tell you weren't from around here."

"And so you wanted to help me find my way?"

"Kind of. You looked sort of lost."

"Perhaps I was."

"And when you asked me for a drink, I was hesitant to accept. Typically, I would never take up such an offer from a complete stranger, but you looked much too lonely and I didn't want you to be so lonely."

"Is that why you're with me now?"

"There's no rhyme or reason for the course of my actions, I was acting out of instinct, and right now my instinct is telling me to make the most of this before it all slips away."

"Like a dream, I suppose."

"I never remember my dreams for more than an instant; I don't think this memory will fade so fast. Your face and the tenderness of your touch are etched into my mind. Not all things pass so quickly."

"Like a waking dream, a dream that never sleeps."

She looked over at me with her wide, gleaming eyes, and with a soft grin, kissed me on the lips, then held me tight. We sat like that for some time, holding each another, warm and happy. My mind was at ease despite the imminence of our eventual parting, but I was content with the present and chose not to depart from the everlasting grace of the now.

As we traveled deeper into the mountains I was overcome with joy, a deep, burning, manic high, over-whelmed by the majestic beauty of the surrounding land-scape and the infinite potential that awaited us in Banos.

We traveled by rivers and lakes, wide expanses of grass and rock, towering peaks etched bald by the persistent caress of wind and water. We stared out into the distance, the shimmering light reflected in her eyes so perfectly delicate and soft, and I wanted to purge myself of these harsh, incoherent thoughts, this unforgiving cacophony of words and sound. I wanted to say, "Don't you see? Don't you see what the world has become? There are no boundaries, no borders, no limits, nothing to deter the famished heart from consuming the everlasting grace of divinity that soaks its warm embrace in our most incidental acts of kindness! There are no walls entrapping our tongues from dissolving ourselves in the most profound utterances that the human imagination can afford! We are infinite in our actions and everlasting in our deeds, we are not the meek that shall inherit the earth, we are the proud and heavy beat of a lion's heart! Don't you see the beauty in all of this? Fate holds no sway; we make it up as we go along."

She looked at me with a kind benevolence, the sort of reassuring gaze that could calm the most ardent soul. Great clarity emanated from those thoughtful eyes, and I was certain she understood without me ever having said a word.

Taking note of her calm demeanor, my thoughts were pacified and my nervous excitement subdued. We held each other in serenity for what must have been an eternity till our eventual arrival in Banos. The city was wide awake, a touristy town set against the background of towering mountains covered in lush vegetation, waterfalls cascading down to the base of the mountainside where the renowned superheated pools waited. We grabbed our bags and headed across the street from the bus terminal, where we were greeted by a young entrepreneur luring us to his family's hostel.

"Cable TV, warm running water, waterfall tours and trips to the jungle."

"How much?" asked Ana.

"Ten dollars a night."

"We'll take it for five."

"Sorry lady, we can't give it to you for five."

"Five's our final offer."

"How' bout seven and we'll give you breakfast in the morning."

"Seven for the two of us?"

"Yeah."

"Alright, take his bag."

The owner of the hostel was an amiable lady standing perhaps five feet with a kind face, and short, curly black hair.

"Is this your husband?" she asked.

Ana looked at me as I nodded my head.

"Yes, as a matter of fact this is our honeymoon."

"Oh, really! Congratulations! I have the perfect room for you; it's a bit more spacious with a Queen Size bed, no extra cost. Anything you need, anything at all, day or night, don't hesitate to ask. Let me get you some towels and show you to your suite."

It was a modest room, but a bargain for the price. Stained wooden walls made it a folksy cabin, with a rather large bed draped in a flower-printed bedspread. It was well into the afternoon by the time we had arrived, but I wasn't quite ready for a night on the town, and was somewhat exhausted from the long bus ride through the mountains. We both collapsed on the bed and stared mindlessly at the stained brown ceiling. I was still riding my manic high through the magnificently carved Andes, stoking passionate and inexplicable thoughts as Ana grasped my hand with a tender touch and turned in my direction, peeking at me like a mischievous child.

"I think I'm falling for you, Jack."

"Well, that's a relief; I fell for you a long time ago."

"But we just met; do you believe in love at first sight?"

"I don't know what I believe, but I don't believe we just met. Souls with similar affinities are drawn together like apple to ground. I just happened to fall from a much taller tree."

"I'm not sure what you mean, but I sense that I've known you for a much longer time."

I smiled as she leaned across the bed and fell on my lips. The sweetness of that mouth was not to be compared to any familiar fruit, but I gladly returned the gesture and felt its supple grasp. I caught a glimpse of her dark flowing hair, bits and pieces of her warm body. In a heat of amorous lust we shed our skin and emptied our hearts. We struck them hard, like two perfectly rounded stones, until they began to spark. Young and foolish, drawn together under a profound bond, our hearts of stone dissolved like melting ice in a cup of warm water and I was sure I was no longer afraid, no more anxious-ridden thoughts or desperate pleas for consolation from the follies of my past. We held tight to each other. I can remember the scent of her perfume and the soft touch of her hips.

After the ecstasy of the moment we lay in each other's arms, naked and silent. As I ran my hand through her hair I noticed a tear running down her cheek, like a single raindrop.

"Why are you sad?"

"I don't know why."

"You don't know why, or you don't want to tell me?"

"Both."

"Well, then tell me why you don't know why."

She took up the corner of the sheet and began to sob, and I could only imagine that she felt ashamed for making love to a man she didn't truly love.

"I know we just met, but there's no shame in having sex."

"That's not it, Jack. It has nothing to do with you."

"If not me, then who?"

She seemed unwilling to divulge the secret of her sadness, but I sensed a truth in her tears and was willing to wait longer than forever if that's what it would take.

"I haven't been with a man for many years. There was only one before you and it didn't work out."

"Listen, I know you think I'm insensitive when it comes to sex, but I've been meaning to tell you something."

"Tell me what?" she asked between sobs.

"*Te Amo!*"

She smiled lightly and began to laugh, "That's cute Jack, but I always sensed you loved me."

"No, but really, I think we can make this work."

"There's always the chance, but I weep not for your loss, but for the past."

"You mean your former lover."

"Jack! When we first met you asked me what I was writing on the computer."

"Yes, I remember clearly, you were surfing the internet, as we are fond of doing in America."

"Yes, but two weeks ago I saw a movie about a thirty-five year old woman that could never have an orgasm, until one day she met a man that touched her heart and dissolved her fear. For the first time she knew how to make love, the ecstasy of sex that I could never achieve. I wept when I saw that movie because I was reminded of the pleasure I could never reach. So, that night when you sat across from me I was reading her story when I noticed you peek from behind your screen--and I sensed the world was a fantastic place where grandiose plots are acted out in the mundane setting of our ordinary lives. I'm crying Jack, not because I think you don't love me, but rather because now I am sure that God has a plan."

"Do you mean..."

"No, but I love you, Jack, as I sense you love me. I am no longer afraid."

I looked at her with mad eyes, mad for love and mad to be loved. I dried her tears and held her tight to my chest. We lay like that for what seemed an eternity as the sky grew dark and the stars unfolded above a city of a thousand lights, above the mountains and the valleys, the rivers and the oceans, the jungle awaiting me just eight hours away, and the people so small they hardly seemed worth the attention. Ana, soft in my arms, naked and secure, made all my troubles appear trivial amongst the great expanse of an infinite universe, boundless in space and just a ripple in time, the fleeting nature of life just an ephemeral shooting star burning up before our eyes.

Ana, having been consoled, sat up in bed and gave me my shot. By now it was too late to go out on the town, but we were content merely to have each other, in no need to hurry our passing moment in time. The dawn would approach the following morning just as it always had. The city would awake, the shopkeepers would open their doors, elderly men and small children would bathe in the pools beneath the mountainside, families would go for long walks along the backstreets as befuddled tourists would stumble out of bed from a drunken stupor the night before. And Ana and I would sleep in, make love and laugh at all those fading stars. I would no longer awake alone, but with the firm and unchallenged sense that we are never alone once we've known love.

I held Ana tight in my arms for fear of losing her in my dreams. Ana turned to me and smiled as though reading my mind through some force of mental telepathy.

"You must let go sometime Jack, but once you know love, you are never alone. Never forget that, and you will never forget me."

I smiled and kissed her on the forehead and fell into a long and silent slumber, forgotten visions overwhelming my senses, only to fade like apparitions amongst the rising dawn. Nothing mattered anymore and I wondered about my trip to the jungle to work with ayahuasca. Was I ready to let go of the past, or had I already let go? For now I was content with the present and chose not to retreat to the past or ponder the possibilities of an uncertain future. Pure electricity crossed the synapses between neurons like small children crossing a stream until they began to dance, to dance up a fiery storm as I drifted off to sleep.

I awoke startled just before sunrise with dreams I couldn't recall. I gently kissed Ana on the shoulder and stepped outside, making my way up a concrete staircase to the roof of the hostel. Dawn would soon approach, as the sun would peek from behind the mountains and shed its skin along the valley floor, but for now the dark was still all-consuming and the stars shown brilliantly, like distant fireflies lighting up the heavens. My dreams were a mystery, but I felt frightened and wasn't sure just why. Perhaps something from my past was still haunting my unconscious mind, some regret about this or that, some hope or dream that had never quite panned out. Then, as I watched the stars shower across the sky, I was overwhelmed by a feeling of pure dread as recollections of my stay on the psychiatric ward came streaming to the forefront of my vision. Lost in the deep, in both space and time, descending into the unknown I had heard a voice from the deep recesses of my mind, not like the dissonance of dialogue that had been battling for my attention, but I realized that there existed some grander force, some last bastion of truth where there appeared to be none. "Know one thing," the voice had said, "know one thing and you can find a way out."

I wasn't sure what that one thing could be. As I trudged my way out of the abyss I held the vision intact and made firm resolve to follow through on my trip to the jungle. The incoherent rant that had been battling for my attention became a single voice leading me in a new and unexpected direction. My one thing now became a destination that lay hidden in mystery just a few hours to the east.

And of course there was the chance encounter with Ana, perhaps through mere coincidence or some form of fate, and last night just before bed I had begun to wonder if she was indeed this "one thing," if I should remain in Banos with her by my side till my eventual departure in just two weeks' time. But what was this dread? What was this nameless fright seething and writhing in the night? Was it the fear of madness? Was it the fear of descending into darkness and never finding truth again? But if I held back, if I quit here and folded my hand, there was no telling what deeper truths I might forego, and perhaps I would never truly understand the secrets of my mind and of my past. Yes! It was folly to hold back, I had been blessed with my time with Ana, but she understood from the very start that one day I would depart, kiss her gently and wave goodbye. All great fortunes come with great risk. Only when you give up everything are you free to know anything.

Light began to filter from across the valley, the lush vegetation along the mountainside gleaming like beautiful emeralds, a mist in the air, a gentle breeze touching my naked skin. The dread could not stand the light of day, and as the stars faded and the moon hid beneath an azure sky, a smile came to my lips and I silently descended from the rooftop and slipped into our room and beneath the covers.

I nestled up next to Ana's warm body, immersed in an alternate reality, careful not to disturb her peaceful slumber, when as though on cue she turned to the side and yawned oh so sweetly, looking me in the eyes with perfect clarity, with perfect contentment.

"How are your balls, *mi amor*?"

"Two things I thought I would never hear in the same sentence, but coming from you it actually sounds romantic."

"So, you're not in any pain from last night?"

"Surprisingly, no."

"Then we can go out dancing!"

"I haven't told you this yet, but I don't dance."

"But I can teach you."

"I'm sorry, I love you deeply, but I don't think any amount of love could teach me how to salsa."

"Please *mi amor*; we only have two nights more."

"Let's wait and see how drunk I get."

"Then you will be too tipsy to learn the steps."

"Yes, but with booze comes confidence."

"I never learned this."

"With my help you will."

"And what shall we do today, this wonderful day in Banos?"

"We shall make love while the stars exhale their final breath, then tramp across town and shower beneath the falls, dip into the scalding baths and wash away our past. Our hearts will beat doubly fast as we pass our way among the winding paths, down into the deep chasms enshrouded by a heavenly mist."

She looked at me with the most endearing smile, still wrapped in flower-printed sheets. "Let the fun begin!" she yelled as she tackled me against the bedpost. We tossed each other back and forth across the bedspread, kissing and playfully biting each other on every part of our naked bodies. While the rest of the town was still in slumber or waking gently for a cup of coffee, Ana and I went at it like two sex-starved animals that had trudged a thousand miles to a watering hole through the desert and overtowering plateaus in hopes of meeting a mate and getting laid. And when the toilet couldn't suck down any more inflated rubber tubes holding enough creative potential to colonize entire galaxies, we unwound in the shower, caressing each other under the trickling warm water and put ourselves back in clothes, to skip blissfully across town to the falls in the distance.

We steeped ourselves in the steaming water that showered into a circular bath from giant fountains. The air outside was still chilly, and although the water would seem a nice change of pace, to move one's body in any direction proved acutely painful even to the most intrepid soul. Alone for a moment we held each other tightly, seated on the underwater bench, until some elderly men came striding in, along with a few audacious foreigners from Western Europe (or so it appeared.) Then, without a moment's notice, a handsome young German man, overly tan and overly muscular, came wooing Ana in a blatantly bombastic kind of way. I liked to imagine that he was boasting of bench-pressing abilities, maxing out on incline with dumbbells at somewhere near two-fifty. I noticed him flex his chiseled pectoral muscles as he said this, only confirming my suspicions. As I laughed inside at his arrogant and self-indulging self-flattery, and what he thought was his unique ability to pick up foreign women, I noted that Ana was laughing at his ridiculous come-on, seemingly smitten by his burly figure and charming speech. Then he departed to the other side of the pool, over to where his buddy of equally bold proportions was eagerly awaiting his arrival, I leaned over toward Ana, and said, "I've noticed that a lot of these German travelers are homosexual. Does he like the design of your bathing suit?"

She smiled, then burst out laughing, putting her hand on my shoulder so as to appease my jealousy.

"No, really! Those guys really know how to party. I saw one strip down to his g-string atop a bar counter one night just down the street from here. I'm kind of amazed that they're actually up this early. They must have skipped breakfast or something."

"He wasn't German."

"Oh, I'm sorry. *Alemán*, then."

"No, he was one of the Dutch, from Holland, where they speak Dutch."

"Oh, them too, those guys are all over each other. Just peek over there, I think those guys are about to Dutch-kiss, it's sort of a gay tradition over there."

She laughed subtly, not at my comment, but at what appeared to be my ridiculous and rather pathetic need to compete for Ana's affection with complete and total strangers (who were obviously not interested in the missionary position, as my suspicions had prematurely confirmed), when she obviously had a good thing going with me. "But did she?" I wondered.

"They wanted to know what we are up to tonight."

"We or you?"

"I assumed we."

"Never assume, that only makes an ass out of you and me."

"So cliché, Jack, they're not after my goods, they just thought that we might want to go out dancing."

"What about our plans?"

"What plans?"

"Heedless disregard for any shred of decency, going buck wild and resurrecting sweet melodies of Eden!"

"Not cliché enough, find some common ground, Jack."

"Ok, ok. If you want to party tonight I'll be glad to accompany you, but don't put your trust in this feller so quickly, the Dutch aren't to be trusted without proper treaties and whatnot. It's almost as if you need to consult the UN with this lot. True party animals, these guys!"

"Will you dance with me then?"

"I'm afraid I might have to, but mainly I'm afraid for the people around me."

"And you won't get jealous of our new friends?"

"You mean your new friends?"

"Yes, I mean my new friends," she responded with an air of annoyance.

"I don't know what you mean. I don't get jealous. I'm open-minded."

"Good then, it will be fun."

"Yes, it'll be a blast, I'm sure of it."

After relaxing for several more minutes in the hot springs, we dressed and meandered among the backstreets of Banos. It was now past noon, as the sun glared down, a few clouds against a deep blue sky, the town humming with activity. We held hands and watched children play in the park; we sat on the swings and pretended to be eight years old again. As we lay in the grass and stared unmindfully up at the puffy cotton balls in the sky I was reminded of my jealousy from just a few moments before. I imagined one of the clouds as a gigantic bicep gently caressing the hair of a beautiful young princess. Then the princess undressed as another hulky cloud came and joined the first bicep as they entangled in a pornographic threesome of heavenly pro-portions. I prayed for a rainstorm, I prayed for a dark cirrus to interrupt and strike at their cumulus orgy with brilliant bolts of lightning.

"Do you see what I see?" asked Ana.

"I hope not."

"Look, there's a turtle and on its back rests the world."

"You mean like the one of Native American myth?"

"Yes, and now the turtle is dissolving and the center cannot hold, we'll all soon be left to the whim of the uni-verse."

"I think the turtle is stronger than you imagine, he doesn't dissolve because he is weak, he appears then disappears so as to conceal his great strength. Yes, perhaps the center cannot hold, but the turtle will carry us, so long as we have faith."

"I believe."

"Believe in what?" I asked.

"In his strength," she said, as she took my hand.

"And if he disappears?"

"Then we must have faith," she said as she pulled me up off the ground.

"I'm very heavy, you must be stronger than I imagined."

"I'm as fierce as the lion; with me you'll never know fear again."

We walked hand and hand through the streets of Banos, a maze of shops and tourist outlets, winding our way through the town center where a giant cathedral was holding morning mass. After breakfast at a local bakery we entered the towering stone structure, through giant doorways into a dark and solemn hollow perhaps fifty feet high. We quietly made our way to an empty pew on the end and took our seats amongst the mass of men, women, and children seated in silence as the priest gave his sermon.

As my Spanish was still hardly fluent I could only make out bits and pieces of his homily, but I took this time to admire the angels hovering above, etched into stone, lurking in the shadows. Images of Christ were pervasive amongst the dark-lit walls, in postures of pain, suffering and then finally redemption. So sorrowful to behold the immense torture that our Lord and Savior must have endured for the sake of all these trifling pieces of flesh seemingly imbued with both mind and spirit, but lost to sin and the dread of the unconscious, only to be redeemed from their follies by the one Son, the great master of all-kind. I recollected my child-hood days, seated at morning mass with my brothers and sisters, not knowing what it was all about, only diverting my attention with trivial amusements. I hadn't attended mass for many years, but now with Ana by my side, holy and devout, and wholly devoted to her faith, I felt an urge to better myself, not to cast grievances at all these little insects and to actually join them in their pilgrimage, to uphold their values and pretend there was a reason behind all the illusions. A reason, I beg you, not for knowing, but sensing beneath the turbulent flux and flow of our words and deeds, a reason for pursuing our path like a dying man breathing his final breath.

When it came time for communion I politely moved aside to let all the devotees amble to the front of the cathedral to eat and drink the body and blood of God's one true Son. When they returned to their seats we all shook hands and kneeled in our pews. I closed my eyes and let the dark consume me, I let the world consume me so as to know my sins, to relieve me of my burden and forgive me for my sinful ways.

"God, if you're listening now, if you ever listen at all, I beg you to hear these words and know them with all the veracity of a child, as if I never knew how to speak words untrue, as if exhaling each syllable like the first breath I drew. Because I have lied and cheated in the past, I have had constant thoughts of envy and lust, of moments of greed and sloth, of words spoken ill of both your Father and his heavenly kingdom. But, I was afraid, as all beating hearts know fear when they cannot see light. And then one night, treading through the abyss I sensed your presence and a silly grin spread across my face. I didn't know then, but I know now. "Know one thing," you said. "Know one thing and you can find a way out." And I was redeemed, and the light spread before me and my fear was appeased, I basked in your radiance and danced myself to sleep. When I awoke the deep was no longer the deep, but the world was born from your tears and painted from your blood. And each day I grew stronger and each night my spirit grew bold. My memory came back in pieces and I could recall my first days beneath the tender touch of my mother's breast. The one thing is not for me to know, it's merely a matter of living for the sake of its pursuit. Perhaps in the end when I have reached the finish I will look back on my days of dread, of sorrow and pain, and you will bless me with your omniscience, and I will know, and all these trifling souls will know the one thing, the only thing worth living for."

I made the sign of the Father, the Son, and the Holy Ghost across my chest as we emptied out of our pews. Ana and I lit a candle in the back, she said a prayer of her own language and nature, as I lit mine and looked to the heavens. She would not divulge the secrets of her heart, but I sensed in her calm demeanor and vital spirit that she had made some amends, or had come to some conclusion. I knew, deep in my heart of hearts, that this was not the typical romance for Ana, a thought which only emboldened my teetering indecision, as I was aware that this relationship, as fleeting as it was, was of a different nature than either of us could have imagined. We had both experienced problems with love in the past, but since our meeting and consequent relationship, every step seemed perfectly fit to the soles of our feet, every beat of our hearts perfectly in sync.

We strolled rather casually through town, eating taffy and joking around, smiling and laughing, not a care in the world, not a wrinkle in the sea. Back at the hostel the young boy from the day before was boarding a jeep to some local waterfalls down the highway. Because it was our "honeymoon," it would be free of charge. Other tourists joined us seated just several rows ahead. The jeep wound its way through Banos and out onto the open road. We marveled at the sights around us, the verdant mountainsides towering above, the deep canyons winding alongside. Graceful waterfalls showered down cliffsides in the distance, dropping hundreds of feet into the mighty river rapidly rushing along the canyon floor. The urge to leap from my seat and down into the river was overwhelming, to rush along with the millions of water molecules to an unknown destination, perhaps out to sea to gather in the wide expansive ocean, to ebb and flow with the tide onto some unspecified, nameless shore. I felt myself embarking on some long, drawn-out journey on a convoluted path that went anywhere but back. And I sensed I was meant for this sort of life. The further I traveled, the more I detached myself from any one soil, from any one heart. But there was Ana clutching to my side, terrified by the precipices portending a possible wreck along the valley floor, and I understood that she had unknowingly seeped into the fabric of my being, and to detach myself was to tear the heart from my flesh and die a lonely death.

This was a disturbing thought--that my very nature, an intrinsic part of my whole value system, had been uprooted. "Why do we feel alone?" I wondered. Why must we surround ourselves with the human race when the human race is a lonely breed? Can't we live like the trees, or fly freely like the birds and all the tiny insects of the world? Can't I be free of all this tiresome affection for people and places, this loathsome, sentimental attachment that burdens the heart, that knowingly deceives itself as though it might just last. But I was happy; I was frightfully overwhelmed by joy with this woman, with this Ana who welled up with tears just feeling me beneath her skin. I wanted more than anything to love and to be loved, but I wanted it to last. Did that mean a lifetime of commitment, of a shared future yet to unfold, a shared past to reminisce about, day by day eking out our livelihoods, bickering over trivial disputes, making amends and laughing at the pettiness and absurdity of what we thought might just matter more than our love. Should we have children and buy a farm, raise livestock and grow row upon row of corn? Shall I tend to fields while she tends to our homestead, break my back and support the young ones so that they may have a future and embark on some sought after dream of some land they have never seen but only heard in stories told around the fire? And will they suffer and will they sin? Will they feel their hearts leap from their chests at the sight of their true loves, only to have their beating hearts torn from their flesh and trampled by time? And will they awake and try once more, and thrive and laugh, and admire the stars, the sky, the open ocean, a wide, expansive horizon with unlimited potential, perils to challenge and treasures to be won? Yes, it seems aimless, so cyclical, but this great truth of life is told time and again through the ages. We pursue the path that suits us best, we feel with our hearts, through the dark and through the light, we trust in God and we trust in ourselves, that we are in fact capable of immortality. Through our actions and told by our tongues, we breed history, we breed poetry, we breed children to fix our mistakes. And this all came crashing upon my burdened head in no less than an instant, in no less than a single blink, a single breath.

We had arrived at the path to *Pailon del Diablo* and my thoughts submerged into my subconscious: yes, I was happy and I was determined to pursue this happiness so long as it was within my grasp. On the one hand, I wanted to detach, I wanted to pursue the path of the ascetic as the shaman had taught me in my sleep, to give up the world so as to revel in the one beyond. But that was merely a possibility, as any number of potentialities exist in our capacity for creating this thing we call life. We are granted, both our burden and our blessing, the infinite creative potential for painting moments and sculpting memories. Ana took my hand as we wandered down the lonely path as the quiet of the forest consumed us, as the roar of the mighty *Pailon* could be heard in the distance. The path was steep, winding back and forth like a ladder unfolding its rungs down into the deep.

Soon enough we had emerged from the forest and reached the sight-seeing station at the mouth of the mighty *Pailon*, its fearsome head showering down in gushing white foam. We paid for admission to the stairway descending down to the base of the falls, then hiked up a solitary path that led us into the heart of its raging fury. Standing there, enshrouded by mist, we posed for a picture with her point-and-shoot camera, then she grabbed me tightly and kissed me deeply.

"I love you, Jack, I love you now more than you will ever know."

"Are you afraid?"

"Not anymore."

"And when I leave?"

"But you haven't left yet."

"And when I do?"

"Then you must promise to come back."

"I promise, *mi amor*."

"Pinky swear?"

"Yes, pinky swear," I said has we locked fingers and cemented our bond.

"Now follow me," she yelled as she quickly descended the precipitous stairway, *Pailon's* breath soaking us to the core. We reached the base where water came showering as if the heavens had opened up after a long drought. Like the land itself, desiccated after years of a scorching sun beating down upon its barren bones, we took great joy in the rain, like small seedlings with parched throats opening wide and reaching out through dense soil only to find that the world is not always dark and silent, and with just the right amount of nourishment the world expands toward a boundless horizon. We took great strength from the falls, holding each other tightly, aware that we would soon depart, but with the promise of a new life. And when we ascended we didn't quite mind being so wet, taking solace in the moment we shared and not shedding tears for doing it just the way we did.

Back up the path, where the jeep had left us, we noticed some small shops of local handicrafts, mainly jewelry made from beads, stones and twine. I noticed two necklaces with the zodiac signs Gemini and Scorpio inscribed on two flat stones.

"What's your sign?" I asked Ana.

"I was born on Halloween."

"Perfect! I will buy us these two necklaces and you can wear mine while I wear yours. They will be our wedding rings to consecrate our sacred vows."

"What vows?"

"Our pinky swear beneath the falls."

"Are you saying you want to be with me?"

"Yes, that's exactly what I'm saying to you."

"Like in a relationship?"

"More like a partnership."

"I don't know what that means."

"It means so long as you wear this necklace, I will be by your side."

We returned to our cabin, necklaces dangling from our necks, our pact solidified and cemented into stone. I think Ana was still itching to go out and dance, but we were both exhausted from our long day in Banos, and we lay still, indolent and disheveled. The night crept in through the windows and Ana asked if I was ready for my nightly shot.

I looked her softly over and pulled down my pants. "Will this be our final one then?"

"Not so quick, you're under my watch till tomorrow night."

"And then my balls will be well again?"

"That's only what we can hope, then you're left to Emiliano. Let him heal your mind, and may you find whatever it is you're seeking."

"The mind can only heal itself. All I ask from Emiliano is

a guide to greater understanding, to reach inside the soft flesh and see it for myself."

"See what?"

"That you will never understand, as I can only begin to imagine, but there await great secrets in the jungle. The medicine is like a pathway into the unconscious, the great unknown finally revealed."

"All that is revealed is what you already know, but perhaps the medicine will remind you of what you have forgotten."

"I only forget what I don't care to remember, but maybe what I don't care to remember is the one thing worth knowing."

"Yes," added Ana, "maybe then you will know one thing."

"That's all I care to know," I wanted to utter, but remained silent as she injected a vial of medicine into my cheek.

"All finished," she said and laid her head along my naked skin, then kissed, then crawled up to lie quietly by my side.

"You'll come back," she whispered in my ear, "I only know one thing, and now that I've found you, you'll never be lost again."

I turned to the side and gently parted her hair behind her neck, leaned in with a kiss, and whispered, "Not all is forgotten."

* * *

We awoke some time later as the town lit up with a thousand electric fires, a heated match of volleyball finally coming to a close in the parking lot across the street, vendors closing up shop and pushing their carts back home, music out in the streets, a vibrant crowd of men and women, families and tourists enjoying the warm breeze blowing through the parks, through the trees and over the mountaintops. Ana's arm lay softly across my chest as my eyes opened, staring at the dark ceiling above. I was hesitant to awake her from her dreams, her chest lifting soundlessly up and down, breathing between her lips like some sweet song of a childhood rhyme. I realized we had one day left, but I couldn't stand the thought of my departure, of our tearful good-bye, our last embrace, our final kiss. I thought of writing a note and sneaking out into the night, stealing away under the cover of darkness, letting her heart beat silently without all the troublesome noise, aching, sorrowful with longing. And as these thoughts came to my mind the sound of awakening, a slight clearing of the throat, like the sound of her soul leaping back into her chest, emerged from the quietude of our cozy cabin. Her eyes opened and blinked several times, her brows arching upward, the skin lining her forehead creased like ripples in a silent pond.

"Jack," she said, "my stomach is angry with me."

"Then we must feed it."

"Where shall we eat?"

"Wherever your heart desires."

"My heart desires nothing more, but my stomach aches for food."

"Then we shall feed it!" I proclaimed emphatically.

She looked at me with an expression of amusement, then began to laugh, sweet bursts of childlike laughter singing soulfully in the night. I grabbed a pillow and smacked her across the head. She stopped laughing as her expression became fierce, but in such a comical fashion that it made me lose my shit, loud cackles of laughter bursting from my lips. She knocked me across the bed and up against the post, holding a pillow across my face in an attempt to suffocate the very source of mockery, like a little girl challenging the seniority of an elder brother.

Smothered in darkness, holding my breath, I patiently

waited for the proper moment for recourse until she let go and retired to the other side of the bed.

"I submit," she said.

"Do you give up that easily?" I asked.

"Not always, but I don't like fighting with you. It's like swimming upstream."

"But I thought you were a lion."

"Yes, and this lion has grown weary of the hunt."

"Then you will starve."

"Yes, then I will starve."

"Then you will die."

"I will not die."

"But we all must die."

"Then we will die together, both the predator and her prey."

"And if you don't eat me then how will I die?"

"Then I will eat you!" she roared, tackling me across the bed and onto the floor, biting her teeth into my neck like a lioness ready for the kill. We rolled back and forth, wrestling along the floorboards, beginning to kiss in a heated passion. She tore off my clothes and I tore off hers, going at it like wild animals, raw and naked, lustful and uninhibited. I sensed something different in this moment, something I had not felt the night before, or earlier in the day. Ana had finally let down her guard and lost herself. I picked her up and pinned her against the wall as she put her hand over my mouth in an effort to control me. A moment of silence ensued, both of us standing naked in the dark.

"Now softly," she said.

I looked into her dark eyes, as my lips gently curved upward. I leaned in as my heart began to pound in my chest, a trembling nervous energy, like great light flowing from my toes to my head. I kissed her on the cheek and then on the lips, moving down her neck and down to her breasts. I laid her on the mattress as her lips curved seductively upward. Unlike before, she didn't grimace with pain. I began to move up and down inside her body. She began to moan, as I moved in and out until finally she pulled me in and we continued to kiss. She tossed me backward onto the bed and climbed on top. She moved up and down, playfully and then more like a pro. I could barely contain myself, seeing her lean graceful figure pump up and down and I began to imagine that if there were a camera, this might be the greatest porno I would ever make. I began to imagine the barren recesses of the Arctic tundra, penguins and icebergs, seals and sea lions. I submerged myself in icy waters, I thought of a polar bear leaping in for the kill. And then, just as hope seemed lost, as if it would devour my entrails and I would no longer be able to stem my semen from launching inside of her, she began to scream in gleeful delight. She shrieked at the top of her lungs, as though to awaken the entire town or perhaps the entire world, and I finally let go. She continued to fuck me until she had grown weary of the kill, then collapsed in my arms and lay silent and warm.

"I'm not hungry anymore," she said.

"Have you lost your appetite?" I asked.

"I ate you," she said, "I've never eaten anyone before, and now I have devoured you."

"I'm glad I was the first, for you will no longer starve."

"Yes, now we may go on living, both the predator and her prey."

"But you ate me, I'm all eaten up."

"I forgive you."

"For what?"

"For not finding me sooner."

"Yes, but now I have found you."

"And you'll never be lost again."

This house, this two-story brown-stained mansion of a house. This acre of grass and a large L-shaped pool in the backyard, surrounded by hundreds of yards of fading grey fence post. Inside live all the tiny people living their tiny lives, watching the little screen flicker with fantastic promises of sought-after dreams. All the pretty people dance and bend to the sound of marketers offering redemption for just one low price. We see through their eyes and we live our lives told by their tongues, live vicariously through all the pretty people that sing and dance to the tune of dollar bills.

My father's eyes are glued to the screen, as the young child sits in his room with all his books and fantasies. He dreams big dreams, of traveling to foreign lands, of sailing across the ocean in pursuit of discovering strange people living in exotic locations. He imagines a world without borders, without walls that impede the body from reaching the other side. He wants to leap into a different sort of screen, one that flickers from the stars and bends its luminescent body down to earth. But he deals in an imaginary world with fictitious people saying fictitious things. His own thoughts get the best of him and enter the realm of his subconscious. He grows older and the voices speak to him at night before he goes to sleep. They speak wonderful things, fantastic, marvelous things that he dares dream. He will be great: he will be the greatest human being that will ever walk the face of earth, ever travel across the sea. His life will be an epic, overcoming impossible obstacles, supernatural forces that stare him down in the heat of battle. He will slay the greatest demons and win the affection of the loveliest women. Treasures will be thrown at his feet, as he lives in idle luxury in great palaces made of stone, towering up on mountainsides overlooking his realm. But what he cannot see is that his greatest foe lives deep beneath the earth, deep within his skull. His fantasies will overwhelm him, take control of his mental faculties and dissolve all coherence, all ability to separate fact from fiction.

They will speak in a thousand different tongues; they will grow sullen and morose. Evil will leak up from the depths of the darkest ocean and seep into the fabric of his being. They will scorn him viciously with every profanity of the earth. Sorrowful lamentations will guide his future, singing regret and the aching sorrow of a life not yet lived. His mind speaks lies, terrible dreadful lies, as he stares in the mirror, listens and nods. There is no redemption from the face of the deep, only great loneliness, bitterness, and tears. He will not walk the earth, hold his head high and cast shadows along the land of his victorious deeds, his lofty meditations, his benevolent manner and haughty disposition. No one will know of his greatness, no one will know of the valor inside his heart that pumps sanguine tears that sing him to sleep underneath the dark shade of a hollow moon.

* * *

Ana not quite awake, I sat still in bed in the deepest shade of darkness just before dawn. Haunted by the past, I was haunted by dreams of a lost age, of forgotten time. My thoughts were beginning to ferment into action; I was over-whelmed with the anticipation of realizing the course of this long and convoluted journey of the heart and mind. I had tasted the medicine just three years ago with little result, abandoning the jungle, jaded and full of regret. My first experience in Montanita with Rodrigo had revived my dream, not quite so vivid and not quite so profound as before, but with just enough magic to prove that my undying quest was not unfounded. I could not have fathomed on that bus ride from the coast just what I could have expected in Riobamba, my encounter with this lovely woman resting by my side, of our promise to forge a future, of the necklaces dangling with hope from the strength of our necks. The moon was almost full, and all the troublesome creatures of the earth were out in the shadows cast by the sharp features of an angular land. They were riddled with purpose; fairies and nymphs dancing beneath the starlight, lending their charms to inert objects, the earth coming to life, as rivers sing lullabies and mighty stones grumble about the days of old. Again, as last night, I wished to depart under the shade of darkness, to shed no tears at the sight of my newfound love fading in the distance. I thought of writing a note and leaving it by the bedside, I thought of quietly packing my bag and running off to the bus terminal. But affection will tie moon to earth, under the force of gravity, as they dance around the solar system, lifting tides and stealing the hearts of many.

Everything made absolute sense at this moment, as it seems when we've found those things that make us happy on the long journey, of sorrows and sufferings, obstacles confronted and overcome, set in place so we are able to reach that shore that we call home. I was home again, beneath these sheets with Ana lying quietly in my arms, I had found happiness, however transitory, but something inside me had changed, my heart had grown strong and I had finally found my sword. Whatever challenges I would face in the week to come, or in the following months and years until I breathed my final breath, would still make sense because I had discovered the will and the fortitude to fight any battle, to slay any demon. The gruesome Balrog from my past still lurked amongst the shadows of my mind, but I was no longer afraid, afraid of attachment or afraid of loss. As Ana had said, "Once you know love you are never truly alone." My heart was aching to change, my heart was no longer afraid.

Ana shifted in bed, turning on her side, opened her eyes and blinked several times.

"I had the loveliest dream," she said.

"Why was it so lovely?" I asked.

"We were just children at the dawn of time, playing in a wide-open field of grass and flowers. Still children, I sensed that we were in love. You tackled me to the ground and we laughed as we watched the clouds. Then a storm came rolling in and the clouds grew dark and grey. Rain from the heavens descended upon us, showering us from above with thick, cold pellets. We were soaked to the bone, but we didn't mind getting so wet. We ran for cover beneath a great oak, huddled beneath its canopy until the storm died down. Then the sun came out and dried the earth and we discovered a great field of water stretching as far as the eye could see. We threw off our clothes and bathed in the shallows, laughing and smiling, concentric circles muddling the water, each ripple an age, each ripple a lifetime. But the world was empty of time and we would never grow old, our skin never wrinkling, our hearts never quitting. And although we were just children, I sensed that I had known you for a very long time, we were mad about each other and all we needed was each other. Death was foreign, decay and ruin mere illusions. The world was at peace, as still as our hearts. And when I awoke just now, the vision still clear in my mind, I realized that this was death; both life before death and life after. Death is just the beginning, just as life is not the end."

I paused for a moment, as she whispered this in my ear; I glanced at her bright eyes piercing through the darkness, her benevolent smile lighting up the world.

"I wish I knew you when we were younger. I wish we had more time together."

"But we will, my dear," I replied.

"How do you know?"

"A promise is a promise."

"Oh yes!" she exclaimed as she tugged on her necklace. "A promise is a promise."

"I didn't want to awaken," she said, "I wanted to play in that field under the bright shining sun till the end of time."

"But time doesn't exist," I replied. "It's all an illusion."

"Yes, but now I am awake and the illusion is not so illusory. We're growing old by the second. Each time your watch beeps, another hour has gone by and we cannot stop your watch from beeping."

"I'll throw it out the window if that's what you desire."

"But it will keep beeping."

"Then I'll crush it with a stone."

"But it will keep beeping."

"Then I'll cast it into the sun."

"Yes but the sun will keep setting, and the earth will dance around its fiery mass, as the years grow old and we wrinkle into prunes."

"That's just our bodies' way of saying it's time to move on."

"But I don't want to move on; I want to stay right here."

"Then we will stay right here and hide beneath the covers. Perhaps no one will discover that we've eluded our ultimate demise."

"Yes, but the sun is rising and we still haven't eaten. We will die if we don't awaken, we will die of a hungry heart."

"This is true, we mustn't hide like worms beneath the soil, we must cast off these covers and embrace the warm air."

"Then we will rise!"

A few moments later we were showered and dressed, meandering hand in hand down the backstreets of Banos to the bakery from the day before. It was early morning and the streets were practically empty, shops just opening, waterfalls in the distance showering down the mountainside. The bakery was closed when we arrived but we could see the owner setting up inside. Ana tapped on the window and in her most pleasant manner asked the kind gentleman if we could order breakfast. Her magnetic smile and charming personality could not be refused, and soon we were seated at our table, glancing at the menu. We ordered some pancakes and sat quietly sipping our coffee when more patrons began to enter, including the two muscular Dutchmen from the baths the morning before.

They noticed us immediately and began to speak with Ana in Spanish. She smiled and laughed, conversing in a light-hearted manner as my jealousy could not be controlled.

"Excuse me," I asked them, "Do you happen to speak English?"

"Oh yes, of course, excuse my rudeness," one of them answered.

"I was just inviting the both of you to come out to some bars tonight."

I stared at Ana, and she stared back with an inquisitive look on her face, as though pleading for acceptance of the offer.

"I'm sorry, my wife doesn't drink."

"Oh," he uttered with a look of disappointment, "I didn't know the two of you were married."

"That's because we're not," she answered him.

I paused for a second, astonished that Ana didn't play along with the charade, and then replied, "Yes that's true, but she still doesn't drink."

"But we must go dancing. Jack, won't you dance with me?"

"But you know I don't dance."

"Yes, but you will learn."

"It's all in good fun," added the Dutchmen, "we just

wanted the two of you to join us."

I paused, collected my thoughts, then replied, "I suppose I will learn to dance."

"Fantastic. We'll meet you in the central park around ten then."

"Surely," replied Ana, then smiled and said something in Spanish as they laughed and exited the shop.

"Can't you see they're hitting on you, Ana?" I exclaimed.

"Oh please Jack, that's nonsense. They're just two friendly travelers looking to have a good time. Don't you want to have a good time?"

"Yes, of course! But with you, not them."

"This isn't really our honeymoon Jack. Let up a little."

"Yes, and you aren't really my wife, but we are together and I don't enjoy you flirting with other men."

"I was merely being polite. That's how I am, haven't you figured me out yet?"

"Apparently not."

"Are you like this with all your girlfriends?"

"I don't know."

"What do you mean, you don't know?"

"I can't remember."

"You can't remember?"

"I've never had one."

We both paused, Ana out of astonishment, and myself slightly embarrassed.

"But what about all those women you've been with? Haven't you ever had a relationship?"

"I can't say."

"You can't say, or you don't want to say?"

"Both."

"Well, either you've had one or not. Which is it?"

"To tell you the truth I don't know what a relationship is like. Do you?"

"I told you that I've only been with one man before you, but I know what a relationship is."

"What does it mean? How can you tell? Is this a relationship?"

"Yes, of course this is a relationship."

"Then why do you want to dance with other men?"

"Relationships are founded on trust and if you can't trust me to be around other men then perhaps you're not ready for a relationship."

A pause.

"It's not that I don't trust you, it's just that I don't want to lose you."

"And how will you control your jealousy when you head back home?"

"I hadn't thought about that."

"Well then, you must trust me as I must trust you."

"Ok, I apologize. I will learn to dance."

Ana smiled as our breakfast arrived. We sat quietly sipping our coffee and eating our pancakes as the town began to hum with activity. Shops were opening, crowds were filling the streets and parks, the sun was rising and the air was growing warm. Once outside I breathed in deeply, cleared my thoughts and discarded my feelings of jealousy. I couldn't be sure what malevolent force was overcoming me. I had never been so in love and I wasn't really sure how to handle myself. Ana was obviously a much more mature human being than I was, but I couldn't understand where she was coming from. Was she a liar? Was this whole relationship thing just a fraud? Maybe she faked the orgasms, maybe she was just conning me into marriage so she could move to the States and leave me for another guy. Hell! Maybe she was a recovering alcoholic, for all I knew. Never had a drink, psss! What twenty-eight year old hasn't had a drink?

But when she took my hand in hers, turned and kissed

me on the cheek I felt right again, looked in her eyes and said, "Let's never fight again."

"I guess you really never have been in a relationship before."

"What does that mean?"

"Honestly, your naïveté is adorable, don't ever wear it out."

"I'll take that as a compliment."

"Bickering is a sign of love. You must really love me."

"I only know what I feel."

"That's probably more profound than you even realize."

"What? Feelings?"

"No. Knowing that you feel things, means you're alive. It means you haven't lost your mind."

"Well, I did once, but then it came back to me."

"Then keep it intact, you'll need it for your journey. Remember we only have a few more hours. How should we pass our final day together?"

"Let's pack lunch, hike into the emerald hills and picnic at the top of the world."

"That's what I love about you, never a dull thought."

"You mean moment?"

"Thoughts aren't moments."

"Yes, but moments are made of thoughts."

"You think too much. Moments should only be made in the absence of thought. Love only happens in the present tense."

"What about desire, what about longing?"

"That's not love, that's merely lust. Be careful not to confuse the two: one's a virtue, the other a sin."

"I think we're having a moment, like an old married couple debating about what to have for lunch."

"Good! There's no thought in that! Now let's stop our squabbling and hike into the rolling hills."

The sun was now rising, tracing its path across the sky towards its zenith as we quietly meandered through town, ducking in and out of local shops, marveling at the workmanship of alpaca cloth and comparing our favorite films, bootlegs for under a buck. I bought a copy of "Eternal Sunshine of the Spotless Mind" for Ana with the intent that we would watch it later in the evening. We passed through the town park, admiring the flowers and playing with the children. We purchased some sandwiches and fruit for our excursion, then headed down a deserted stretch of road toward the trailhead that lead up into foothills encompassing the city.

The path was gentle and steady at first, growing steeper with each step forward. We hiked patiently upward, following a narrow dirt trail punctuated by stones and roots, bending and contorting its snake-like pathway along the crest of a rising peak. My heart began to beat faster, as the blood in my veins pumped more vigorously, my lungs struggling for oxygen, my breath heaving inward and outward like that of a man not accustomed to physical activity.

"I should really quit smoking," I said.

"I didn't mention anything before, but I wish you would."

"It's a bad habit."

"We're creatures of habit, we live our lives entrenched in routine. You need to find something new, find something you love and let it love you back."

"Like woodworking?"

"Like anything that improves your life rather than taking it away."

"Maybe I should take up a craft; I could carve necklaces out of *tagua* and then sell them to tourists for an exorbitant amount of money."

"Look down at the city," she said as we climbed upward into the surrounding hillside. "Look how small we all look when seen from above."

"Like tiny ants, insignificant insects looking for leaf scraps to carry back home."

"Is that a metaphor? Or do you really think of us as nothing more than ants?"

"I don't know, I used to think that way."

"Do you think ants dream? Do you think an ant could invent the airplane, the automobile, the microchip?"

"I thought you said that dreams were meaningless."

"I'm beginning to reconsider."

"And what changed your mind?"

"I'm not sure, but that dream from last night was so vivid, so real. Normally they fade so fast, but something's changed, I think my dreams are trying to tell me something."

"My dreams always tell me something, and right now I think they're telling me to move forward."

"Instead of running in circles?"

"Perhaps they're telling me to break the mold, the habit of the heart to remain bitter and alone. I had a dream of the jungle the other night: a fearsome shaman of ancient lore told me to give up on this world and embrace the one beyond."

"You mean like an afterlife?"

"I'm not sure, but I'm not ready to give up on this world, I've grown accustomed to my habits."

"There's nothing wrong with breaking bad habits, perhaps the shaman of your dream was just letting you know it's time to change."

I smiled as we reached the top of the hillside. We both paused to catch our breath; we sat atop a giant boulder and peered down across the valley while eating our sandwiches. From up here Banos looked so small, so fragile, so trivial.

"Looking down from above sure gives a man perspective, lets him know that as deep as his problems may run, they have no relevance in the grand scheme of things."

"And what's the grand scheme of things?" asked Ana. "Don't you think that we create our own meaning, that our problems are the very same problems of the world, that together we strive to improve ourselves and through our deeds we transform the earth?"

"I just mean that the universe is so vast, seemingly infinite in both time and space, and that unlike ants we assign meaning to our actions when the outcomes really have no relevance; we're all just turning like cogs to keep the machine running smoothly, to keep chaos at bay."

"It's called entropy, Jack; it's the law of the universe. To avert disaster we must put things in order."

"Yes, but I just wish we could live like this always: feet on the ground, head in the clouds. If we carried this perspective we wouldn't get so unsettled about the minor upsets of a worldly existence and we might be better off for it. Perhaps we'd be kinder; perhaps we'd be more human."

"Humans can't live in the clouds, Jack. We are the eyes and ears of God, we suffer so that we may learn important transformative lessons, we live so that we may teach our spirits to be bold in battle, yet meek in triumph. And when we reach a crossroads we will know which path to follow because our pasts were not in vain, our lives were not without aim, not without purpose."

"Yes, but even cogs have purpose. What's the difference?"

"Because unlike cogs we can reflect, and unlike cogs we have free will."

"Do you have free will to leap off this mountainside?"

"I do, but that wouldn't prove anything. That wouldn't teach me anything but not to leap off mountainsides."

"So, you act within boundaries, you act out of reason. Do you think that we're all just slaves to reason?"

"It's not a reasonable thing to be in love. Do you think that a cog knows the joy of love?"

"I don't think that cog-love is all that different from human-love. With each rotation, cogs yearn to touch to cogs below and above them, and with each retreating clasp a new clasp is formed so that they are never alone, so that out of yearning chaos is averted, the machine keeps running, and the universe remains intact. Perhaps love is the one true law of the universe, the law that binds the wounds of man and cog alike."

"Yes, but a wounded cog will never be complete, and a wounded man will never be healed if he doesn't overcome his passions, if he doesn't learn that love isn't about yearning, it's about being part of something that's bigger than yourself--knowing that you're not alone even when no one's around, knowing that your every action has meaning, that your words are not silent when you speak."

I looked over at Ana perched on the edge of the boulder overlooking the vast valley draped in greenery, the small town of Banos humming with activity hundreds of feet below, the air gliding smoothly across our skin, completely aware that soon we would depart, the wind would die down and the skies would grow quiet.

"I think I've been silent for a long time now, I'm glad I'm a part of you."

"I don't think you've ever been silent Jack. I think you're just learning that you have a voice and that your voice speaks volumes."

Then she moved toward me, grasped my head in her hands and kissed me deeply on the lips, held me tight and stroked my hair as if to let me know that everything would be alright, that as the world turns, so do we.

"Should we venture onward or are you ready to descend, to return down to the order of cogs?"

"The afternoon is wearing on. Let's make this count!"

* * *

"Are you ready?" asked Ana, a vague shadow of a woman lying beside me in the dark of our cozy cabin, moonlight gently peeking in through the window, casting shadows against the wallpaper.

"Is your stomach angry with you?"

"My stomach is full with hunger."

"Then this will be our final meal together?"

"Don't say it like that, you sound so sullen. This should be a night of celebration, a night to remember!"

"I'll come back, and when I do I will know you all the better."

"Yes, you will know one thing and you'll have no reason to leave."

"I can't fathom how I'll return to something so mundane after experiencing something so extraordinary."

"Take your lessons learned and incorporate them into your daily routine. Remember what I said: Find something to love and let it love you back."

"But I've already found something to love."

"And it loves you back."

"Then come with me. I'll get you a visa."

"Even if you could, my life is here and your life is there. I have roots in Riobamba as you have roots in Jersey."

"What roots?"

"You have family and friends; you have a job and school to tend to."

"Mere diversions. I have no roots. I pulled them from the soil a long time ago."

"Then you'll never grow branches or sprout leaves to blossom into flowers, you'll never know the joy of weathering the winter, only to realize that spring is on the horizon."

"Yes, but I will know the seasons in a thousand different shades of light, I will watch the sea ebb and flow along a thousand foreign shores. I will make friends of strangers and share the passing of an age with an entire race."

"And you will let friends become strangers and watch a race suffer and lie sallow as you neglect your one true duty."

"And what would that be?"

"They say the greatest things in life can't be expressed in words, but when you find the words, the world listens. Find the words to express the inexplicable and you have found the one thing worth knowing."

"I'll come back."

"I trust you will."

We quietly slipped out of bed and dressed, locked the door to our room and prepared for our final night together in Banos. As we went out the hostel entrance, the owner greeted us from inside the café.

"Will you two be leaving in the morning?"

"Yes," said Ana, "we've enjoyed our stay, but it's time to head back home and start our lives together."

A subtle smile traced her lips, "And are you thinking of having children any time soon?"

"We haven't thought about it," I told her, "but it's certainly something to think about."

"Marriage is a beautiful thing," she told us. "Trust in yourselves and trust in each other, and when that time comes, raise your children with the same love and tenderness that you hold in your hearts. The rest will follow. Although my husband has passed, I raise my children knowing his love. Cherish this moment because this is all you have, this is all you will ever have. The youth will become the elderly and the elderly will pass away, but so long as we continue the dance the world will go on living."

We both thanked her kindly and said our goodbyes. The night was now well underway, the moon nearly full, the stars brilliantly decorated the vast abyss of darkness enveloping the earth on its path to a new day, another chance to awake, and another chance to rest our weary heads in sleep.

Down in the heart of town the world was alive, couples young and old, families and travelers congregating in the park, in and out of cafes and restaurants, listening to music and laughing loudly under streetlamps. Against Ana's wishes I purchased a bottle of red wine from a local shop as we passed from spot to spot, reading menus and comparing meals.

"Choose whatever your belly desires. I want this night to be special."

"Really Jack, it doesn't matter. Food is food. I'd be happy with a burger if that's what you want."

"No really, I want this to be perfect. Whatever you want, it's all on me."

"Really Jack, I can pay for myself. Save your money for the jungle."

"Trust me, Ana, when you look back, this is what you'll remember. It's entirely up to you."

"It's just dinner, Jack. Meals come and go. I'll remember a lot more than some pasta."

"So, would you prefer Italian?"

"Pizza's fine."

"No, pizza's not fine; your folk don't know a thing about pizza. How bout Mexican?"

"You mean tacos?"

"Ok, how about steak?

"Steak's fine," she stated rather obstinately.

"Alright then, perhaps seafood?"

"Really Jack, it doesn't mean a thing; we could eat taffy

114

for all I care."

"We haven't eaten since this morning! Aren't you hungry?"

"Yes, but I want you to be happy, so just choose something you like and we'll eat."

"I'll be happy only if you're happy."

"Ok, how about chicken?" she suggested as we passed a fast food place on the left.

"Fast food? Wine doesn't go well with fried chicken."

"I don't want wine. I don't drink! Remember?"

"Just a little won't hurt."

"No!" she exclaimed, "I don't mind if you have a drink, but I'm not going to join you."

"Must you always be a saint?

"God! It has nothing to do with being saintly. I just don't drink. Understand?"

"Ok, ok, let's eat burgers then!"

"Don't raise your voice with me; I'm just trying to make you happy."

"Are burgers not alright?"

"Burgers are fine; everything we've seen so far is fine, let's just get this over with!"

"Jeez, why are you so upset all of a sudden? This isn't like you. What's the matter?"

"What's the matter? You're asking me what's the matter?"

"Yes."

"You expect everything to be so damn perfect! Well, it's just a meal and it's not always going to be perfect, we're not always going to be perfect. I wanted this evening to end on a high note and you're ruining everything with your..." Then she trailed off, muttering something in Spanish, something that sounded a lot like profanities.

"Alright, alright, let's just eat here. They have pasta and

burgers, and I see candles inside. It doesn't have to be perfect, I just want you to be happy. I just want our final meal together to be something special."

Still angry with me, she began to walk off across the street and into the park.

"Ana!" I yelled. "Ana! Ana! Come back, it doesn't matter. What the hell are you doing!? Where the hell are you going!?"

I ran across the street and grabbed her by the shoulder.

"Get your hands off me!"

"Why? What's gotten into you?"

"Please Jack. I just need some time alone."

"Please come back, it doesn't matter, the food isn't important. Let's just resolve this thing and have some dinner."

"Not like this, not with you being so damn…"

"Please Ana, I don't want the night to end this way. Let's just eat at this Italian place and gather our wits."

She stood still with her hands folded across her chest, hesitating in a bitter silence, then obstinately trudging across the sidewalk, angry and resentful.

"A table for two," I told the hostess as we entered the restaurant. She seated us in the corner of a room, empty except for the company of a lone family.

We sat in silence, both sulking in our bitterness. I couldn't understand what had come over her, why she felt so hostile, so resentful at my mild attempt to be romantic. She sat still, looking away into the corner, not even attempting to recognize my presence. I was upset, but I wanted to reconcile our differences so as not to taint this final evening. I decided to wait and not disturb, to give her space and not disturb her distraught disposition. The wound would heal itself, I thought. She'll come around when she needs to.

I opened the wine bottle and poured myself a drink.

I sat.

I sat.

I sat.

I drank.

I drank.

I drank.

"Are you going to get drunk?" she finally muttered.

"Possibly."

"You really shouldn't drink alone, that's what alcoholics do."

"Are you suggesting that I'm an alcoholic?"

"No, but you could be. I don't know. I don't know anything about you."

"Why do you say that? How could you say that? You know everything about me."

"I didn't know that you drink alone."

"Then drink with me."

"Maybe you don't know anything about me."

"I know you don't drink."

"Then why do you ask?"

"Because circumstances have changed."

She looked me over as I sipped my wine, a biting trace of resentment stirring on her brow, then she grabbed the bottle off the table and poured herself a drink.

"See," she announced, as a sly smirk crossed her lips, "you don't really know anything about me."

"I know that if you've never drunk, you'll be drunk by the end of that glass."

"What do you care? You want me to get drunk."

"I don't want you to do anything you don't want to do. I just feel that you need to lighten up a little, maybe drink wine occasionally, maybe smoke a cigarette, maybe fall in love, maybe lose yourself."

"The way you lost yourself?" she said as she began to

laugh, a trace of sarcasm on her breath. "Then who will find me? I'll have to find myself I suppose. That's all I'm good for."

She sipped some of her wine, then began to relax. "You know, I should have known you were trouble from the start when you asked me where to get a drink."

"And I should have known what I was up against when you told me that you don't drink."

"And is this more to your liking?"

"Well, yes, please drink and lighten up a little. Let's put this little tiff behind us and set things right. I just wanted to enjoy a romantic evening together; I'm just trying to be a gentleman."

"Yeah, but you're trying way too hard. I don't need all this extra attention, Jack. I'm a simple woman with simple tastes. I don't need wine and candles or expensive Italian food. You don't have to go off on this grand adventure, you know. We could just spend some more time together."

"Ah, I see. So, this is really what this is all about. You don't like the idea of me fulfilling my dreams."

"What? That's not it at all. I don't care what you do. I'm just saying that you don't have to be so damn grandiose, like the earth is going to fall to pieces if things don't turn out the way you planned."

"And things never do."

"That's just the way things work. This is life and life is far from perfect. You accept circumstances and deal with them. If you don't learn to cope you're going to fall to pieces."

"I'm coping, I'm coping right now. I told you already, I don't know what a relationship is supposed to be like. I'm learning as I go along. I'm learning the hard way at a very late stage in my life. Cut me a little slack. Let's just try to learn together."

She took another sip of her wine and then began to chuckle. "Isn't this perfect? Aren't we a pretty pair?"

Then, in the midst of our reconciliation, a pair of musicians walked in, a pretty young woman and a young man with long hair and a guitar. They discarded their jackets and the man began to strum a few chords while the woman began to sing. Her ballad was soft and soulful, an old Latin love song that spoke of a broken heart. Her voice would rise, then fall, each note more sorrowful then the next.

Ana took a sip from her glass as her eyes welled up with tears. Sitting across from her, the candle flickering in the dark, her sobs growing strong, I was overwhelmed by emotion, and I couldn't help but cry as well. We sat there in silence, wrenched with sadness as we both understood that the dawn would soon approach and we would pass our separate ways.

I handed her my napkin as I attempted to pull myself together, both of us a mess of tears, a mess of ourselves. After a few minutes of quiet sobbing, we both began to laugh in the subtle realization that we were both being immature, making something out of nothing, nonsense out of nonsense.

Ana had by now nearly finished half her glass as her laughter grew louder, and her smile opened wider. Through the catharsis found in tears, I smiled as well, not realizing the poignancy of the moment, not realizing that I was living in the present tense. There were no more thoughts, no more tears, no more anxiety or fear. Joy leaped up from my chest and I began to understand the strength of our bond. Tonight Ana would give me my final shot and my balls would be healed. I would be free to undertake my endeavor, to follow my heart to its final destination.

The waiter came and took our order as I poured myself another glass of wine. Ana took another sip. I could sense that she was getting drunk.

"Yes, a pretty pair indeed, I believe we've made a mess out of nothing and out of nothing comes something, maybe even something greater than ourselves."

"So, are we better than cogs?"

"Is cog-love so bad? Maybe together we can tell time, maybe apart we can keep the dial in motion?"

"But I thought you said time didn't exist, that it's all an illusion."

"Remember your dream, remember the open meadow and the still pond. Our actions are nothing but concentric ripples starting at a single point and expanding outward in all directions until they reach the shore and come rippling back inward. But the whole time the pond was still, and when we quit, when we stop breathing, the pond will sit silent waiting for another pebble. Our job is nothing more than to keep tossing pebbles and let the ripples come back from shore and meet us in the middle."

"You and all your talk of pebbles, am I nothing more than a pebble to you?"

"What matters is not your pebble-ness, but the fact that you're the right pebble at the right moment."

"We certainly are making a mess out of this pond."

"It all comes back, it always does."

Our tears dried along the tablecloth and the sleeves of our shirts, and as they dried we sipped our wine and listened to the fading sounds of this poor woman's broken heart. But in the end she found the pieces and set them right. It seemed that Ana and I had resolved our first real fight, but I still pondered the deeper wound that invoked so much bitter-ness, a side I had never seen in her.

"And when I leave in the morning will you head back to your chickens waiting to be fed? They must be hungry by now."

"My mother looks after them, but we're looking to sell.

My parents are separated and we're looking to move."

"And where will you move?"

"A smaller, more affordable house, a smaller house with no room for chickens."

"They must be sad knowing that the chickens will soon be food."

"Yes, but tasty food nonetheless."

"And you feel no remorse? Aren't they your friends?"

"Like I said when we met, the world is a cruel place. Don't ever think otherwise."

"Yes, but in its cruelty something beautiful arises."

The waiter came with our meal, and the melody in the background grew from melancholy to whimsical, elevating the mood and lightening our hearts. I was no longer sorrowful, afraid to leave behind my one certainty. Rather, my spirit grew bold and I felt anxious to leave it all behind in pursuit of the great unknown, the long-sought truth buried beneath the earth, beneath my skull. The last bastion of truth, something long forgotten, was awaiting me behind the towering sculpted peaks just several hours to the south. The anticipation was palpable and I sensed that Ana was just as much a part of me as I had become of her. Although our paths were separate they were leading in the same direction, and when I was through with the ordeal or whatever messy adventure awaited me off on the horizon, my certainty would solidify and our tiny hearts of stone would continue to spark, lighting up the earth, passing through the dark.

* * *

Meandering beneath the streetlamps, hand in hand, arm in arm, slightly intoxicated and slightly out of our wits, ten o'clock was soon approaching and we were on our way to the park to meet the Dutchmen. The Dutchmen, may I add, whom I wasn't very fond of meeting and whom I secretly felt were trying to thieve the very object of my affection. But to be a man about it, I felt I needed to prove to Ana that I wasn't the jealous type and was perfectly alright with her dancing with other men. And to be honest about it I was terrified of the prospect of dancing in a crowded club around other, vastly more skilled dancers who would certainly mock me for my awkwardness and send me back to junior high.

To my chagrin the Dutchmen were right on time, wearing gaudy shirts and tight-fitting slacks, revealing more of their anatomy that I cared to be aware of. They greeted Ana in Spanish and kissed her on the cheek.

Thieves!

Scoundrels!

Usurpers!

Head back to Holland and whittle yourself some wooden shoes!

"I'm sorry, I didn't catch your names at the bakery this morning," I welcomed them.

"This is Samuel," said the one from this morning, motioning to the one with long, curly blonde hair, "and my name is Eric."

Eric was the taller of two, with short, carefully cropped brown hair and a bit of facial stubble. Samuel was the more handsome of the two and slightly more reticent. In all truth, I was concerned about both of them, and I aimed to make these concerns quite vocal.

"Pleasure to meet you. I'm Jack and this is Ana. We've had a long day so I don't figure we'll be out too late. I have a bus to catch in the morning."

"Oh, you'll be fine, my dear," said Ana, somewhat off-balance and with a bit of a slur. "You'll be fine, we'll be fine, Sammy, we just had some wine and I'm ready to do some dancing."

"Oh, we understand," said Samuel. "We've had a long day ourselves. Did some rafting down the Napo into Puyo. Class IV rapids, a bit of an adventure."

"Is that the highest class?" asked Ana.

"No, not the highest," stated Eric, "but not for novices."

"You two must be very brave."

"I wouldn't say that, but it was tiring nonetheless." "So, where are we heading?" I asked, attempting to be curt, not even slightly interested in rafting or rapids, and slightly concerned that Ana might be a little too drunk to hold herself together.

"There's a cool little club around the corner called *La Cascada*. Cheap drinks and good music. I think you'll like it."

"Well, let's get started!" exclaimed Ana, "Do you know how to salsa, Samuel?" she asked, as she took his hand and began to dance.

"I'll do my best," he laughed, taking her hand, two steps in, two steps back.

I quickly worked my way in between them and put my arm around Ana's shoulder.

"She's had some wine tonight. I'm not sure she'll be sober enough to salsa."

"Oh Jack, my darling Jack, don't be so jealous. I'll teach you the steps."

"Yes, but you've never had wine before. I must first teach you how to step. Lean on my shoulder and focus your feet, one in front of the other, like this," I demonstrated.

"And to think this is what I've been missing all my life. I'm glad you got me drunk. I feel liberated!"

"Liberated isn't the word. On second thought: gentlemen, I think we'll be heading back to our room. I think Ana might want to sleep this one off."

"That's up to you," responded Eric, "but really, I think she'll be fine. How much did she have to drink?"

"Just one glass, but she's never drunk before."

"Please Jack, don't baby me. We'll be fine. You don't have to dance if you don't want to, but we're going to have a great time."

"Alright, just for an hour or so, but I don't want you drinking any more, all right?"

"That's it, my love. Please, please, let's just loosen up and enjoy ourselves."

"This is it, right over here on the right." Eric motioned to a well-lit bar with loud Latin music emanating from inside.

"Fantastic," said Ana. "Now let me show you a good time."

We opened the doors and the music grew louder, a wide-open dance floor with a few couples getting started, tables packed with travelers, a long L-shaped bar crowded with young people drinking beers and conversing loudly beneath the hum of "*Gasolina.*"

"Doesn't this song ever go out of style?" I mentioned to Samuel. "It seems like they've been playing it for the past three years."

"Maybe even longer, but it's better than salsa. Can I get you guys a drink?"

"Sure, a pint of Imperial should do, but don't let Ana have any more, she's not accustomed to alcohol."

Samuel and Eric grabbed some barstools and settled into the mix, as I grabbed Ana's hand and yelled into her ear, "I may not know how to salsa, but this I can dance to."

Ana smiled and laughed, took my hand, began to jump up and down, twist her hips and spin around. I let the music course through my veins, feel its rhythm, then began to move to the music, to let Ana lead my body back and forth.

"Let go of your hips!" she yelled. "Don't be so uptight! Put your hands on my waist and loosen up a little."

I let my body go limp and let her hands guide my waist.

Ana smiled and laughed. "Now that's the Jack I love!"

Soon the song ended and Samuel was back from the bar. He handed me my beer and I quickly took a swig.

"You're getting the hang of it, Jack," said Ana. "You just need to loosen up a little. You're too rigid. Maybe you should drink some more."

"Yes, but then I'll be too tipsy to learn the steps."

"With booze comes confidence. I'm slowly learning that."

I took my beer to the bar and ordered a round of shots for me and my friends. "So when's it back to The Netherlands?" I asked Eric.

"Just a few more days. I'm an airplane pilot. I travel all over the world, but it's not often I meet a girl like yours. You're a lucky man; I just hope you realize how lucky you are."

"She's looking to get a position with the Embassy. Do you have any connections?"

"Yes, she mentioned that, but even if I did, would you really want that for her?"

"I just want her to be happy, wherever or with whomever she chooses."

Eric smiled and patted me on the back. Then we all took our shots of tequila and raised them above our heads.

"To good friends and good times!"

"Cheers!"

We all downed our drinks, then licked the salt off our hands and bit into our limes. Some loud salsa music came on as Eric took Ana's hand and began to dance. Samuel was busy talking to some fellow Europeans in the corner, as I turned to the bar and ordered another shot. For one thing, I felt I could use some confidence on the dance floor and although no longer jealous of the Dutchmen, I wanted to show Ana another side of myself, a playful, spontaneous side, one that could evoke jealousy in the hearts of onlookers, one that told Ana that I could live up to all her expectations.

The next shot left an acidic burning taste in my throat, scorching down my esophagus; then I ordered another. As I did so a pretty American girl with blonde hair and blue eyes sat next to me.

"Your girlfriend is beautiful. Aren't you worried?"

"I think it's not that I'm not worried, I've just slowly forgotten what it means to be worried."

"It means that if you don't keep an eye out you may be heading home alone."

"I may head home alone, I may head home broke and wasted, but my will is not to impose any will, if you know what I mean. If you come with nothing and leave with nothing then I suppose you haven't really lost anything."

"And what if you come with something and leave with nothing?"

"No one ever comes with something."

"Mind if I buy you a shot?"

"Now you're onto something," I said as I put down another tequila, winced and bit the lime.

"A toast," said the girl as she raised her glass. "May we all come with nothing and leave with something. It's the only sure bet."

"Cheers!" I exclaimed as we touched our glasses and let the burning sensation swallow our fears. The salsa music died down and transitioned into a Latin love song. Ana grabbed another guy as I turned to the blonde. "Care to dance?"

By now I had already had too much too drink, and as my concerns about Ana washed away, so did my concerns about embarrassing myself on the dance floor. Young couples spread throughout the bar and all I could remember was a sad voice fading in the distance:

Una noche te irás
Y me quedo pensando
Una noche te irás
Y me llena de lágrimas

Por qué te vas
Por qué te vas

Nos encontramos por casualidad
Y me quedo pensando
Ni siquiera bailamos
Y ahora bailo solo

Por qué te vas
Por qué te vas

Todos mis deseos van contigo
No sé nada
No sé nada

Estaba tan lleno de esperanza
Y no sé nada

Te vi en la distancia
Y no pude decir nada
Nos estamos quedando sin tiempo
Y no pude decir nada

Me olvidarás
Me olvidarás

Si te vas, recuerda
Tienes mi corazón

Si te vas, recuerda
Te amaré siempre

Por qué te vas
Por qué te vas
Por qué te vas

Mañana saldrá el sol
Y yo estaré esperando
Esta noche la luna está creciendo
Y yo estaré esperando

Por qué te vas
Por qué te vas
Por qué te vas

Assailed by darkness, lost to the deep. My body was burning and my head was throbbing with indescribable pain, with a loud, pounding beat that would not quiet, even when surrounded by silence. I leaned my head up against the window, but I could barely make out the passing scenery beneath the shifting moonlight. My breath still tasted of tequila and I sensed I was still intoxicated. A loud scream from a frightened child interrupted the silence like a dagger in my spine, ominous in a way, foreshadowing death, reeking of desperation.

The bus moved slowly over the broken pavement as we wound our way down out of the Andes and into the Amazon Basin. I wasn't really aware of all this at the time, just that something had gone terribly wrong, that I was on my way to somewhere dark and everything in the past was long forgotten. The silhouette of a man slowly made its way down the aisle, stopping every few feet to converse with the passengers. When he reached my seat I ignored his presence and tried to console myself by staring out the window.

"Ticket please?" he asked in Spanish.

"What?" I responded.

"I need your ticket."

"I don't have one."

"Five dollars please."

I reached through my pockets and luckily found my wallet. I opened it up, but it was empty of cash.

"Can I pay when we arrive?"

"No, I need your five dollars or you'll have to leave."

"Well, I don't have any money."

"Then you can't ride any farther."

He quietly continued down the aisle collecting tickets, as I attempted to recall just where I was or how I got here. I remember sitting across from Ana at a lone table in a dark room lit by a single candle. There was music, beautiful, soulful music clouded by desperate tears.

"Why did you leave me?" she whispered in my ear.

"Because you asked me to," I responded.

The bus continued onward into the darkest shades of night. The land was beset by all the troublesome creatures of the earth, running around beneath the stars, lending their magic to the sorrows of all the tiny people, lending their ears to all those who would speak without fear. The moon was waxing to its completion, lighting a path for all those that would follow. Soon enough, the bus came to a halt in a small town in the foothills of the Andean Cordillera, and a man showed me out the door as I stumbled, inebriated and sorrowful.

A few men and women exited as well. As they trailed off down a dirt path towards the town, I asked in a low tone, "Where are we?"

"We're here," responded the short silhouette of an old woman, a potato sack hunched on her back, "Where are you?"

"I don't know."

"Well, another bus will come. Just wait and it will come."

Then she continued trudging slowly toward a mass of small wooden shacks huddled on a hillside overlooking a vast forest of trees swaying in the breeze. So I huddled as well on a small wooden bench as the cold sent shivers down my spine. I reached in my pocket and uncovered a pack of cigarettes. Luckily I still had some matches, so I lit one up and tried to recollect. And as I exhaled the smoke, I felt an overwhelming urge to vomit. I stood up and bent over, leaning up against the back of the bench until I puked up a putrid mess of alcohol and Italian food. Memory from the night before arose from the dark.

There was a sad song in a crowded bar and I was dancing with a pretty girl. I was drunk and out of my wits. We came close and we nearly kissed. But I refused and kept dancing. Out of the corner of my eye I caught a look from Ana, the true object of my affection. She was with that Dutchman, the taller one with the short brown hair. And as she caught my glance, she stood up on her toes and kissed him on the lips. I was furious with rage, my heart pumping, boiling red blood. Without a thought I ran over and broke them up. He looked at me in astonishment, and I yelled at the top of my lungs above the hum of the sad song. He pushed me back and I took a swing, hitting him dead center on the jaw. He fell backwards against the wall, then came swinging until he knocked me on the lip. I hit him back, knocking him to the floor, a bloody mess of broken flesh.

"Get out of here!" yelled Ana. "Get out of here and never come back!"

I trudged out the door and meandered in a drunken haze back to the hotel. I grabbed my bag and prepared to leave, to leave and never come back. But as I left a thought took hold of my bitter tears, my resentful, angry tears, and I left the necklace hanging from the doorknob.

"No one comes with something," I thought, "but sometimes he leaves with less than nothing."

* * *

I sat patiently and waited. I waited an hour and then another. I waited as the night grew lighter and the air grew warmer. And as the soft rays of the sun began to peek around from the other side of the earth I curled up on the bench by myself, with myself and nothing more.

I awoke at dawn to the loud sound of a chiming bell from somewhere in the east amongst the huddled shacks, the desperate, crowded mess of wood and tin, of misery and squalor. As I awoke the sun was rising along the eastern horizon, peeking out from above the lush green hillside. Having purged myself earlier I was now in dire need of nourishment. My stomach growled with anger, so I was left with no other option but to seek out help from the villagers of an unfamiliar land.

As I made my way along the dirt path leading into town I made note of women and children scurrying about in their best-dressed attire. I couldn't recall the day as my mind was all a haze, but I inferred that it must be Sunday, the day of rest, and morning mass was about to begin. I stumbled now and again, a crooked gait for a crooked man, but as I walked my headache diminished and my hangover retreated.

For the most part, the villagers ignored my presence, except for the subtle glances of small children pulling on their mothers' dresses and pointing in my direction. I occasionally waved or greeted them *"Buen día,"* but it would seem that I was a bizarre spectacle at such a time of day, walking rather clumsily by myself without any possessions. Then, rather abruptly, toward the base of the hillside I noticed a small stone building in the shape of a church, a modest spire ringing for the final time. It was now seven o'clock and the town was alive.

As I entered I was rather surprised--delicately carved pews of stained finished oak, images of saints hanging along the wall, the priest standing before his flock along the raised altar, a crowd of men, women and children listening intently to the day's sermon. He spoke with grave solemnity, in a loud and forceful tone, and although my Spanish wasn't quite adequate to understand every word, I knew this man was a man of God. I listened intently as I closed my eyes. I let the words overwhelm me and carry me away from the troubles at hand. As he concluded, the crowd began to sing. Through their song I repented f o r my sins, kneeled on the floor, hands clasped in prayer, I decided that today was a new day, a day to be born again.

"I do not know man and I do not know God. I only know that I know nothing at all. But if I were to know anything I would know man and I would know God. I would know one thing and I would no longer be lost. Like my heart my words have been silent for a long time now, and like the caterpillar buried in its cocoon it is time that my heart awaken and take flight from its duress, fly far away and never look back. The wrath of the heart is a troublesome creature when it does not know temperance, when its greed knows no bounds, when its thirst can not be quenched, its hunger not sated. I speak without syllables, I speak without words, my voice speaks volumes and now I beg you to listen. If there is any mercy in your soul and if there is any mercy in my soul and the soul of the world, I will repent and in revealing my sins, I will be redeemed and know the light again, the light that first struck in the darkest shades of dawn. Show me one sign that I am not alone. Show me the path to my final destination and secure my journey, and I will believe, I will have faith."

And as I ended my prayer the song came to an end. The mass continued as I sat in silence and listened to the sermon, making out a word or two, but never fathoming the full breadth of its intent. I glanced at the solemn faces, the hard weather-beaten faces of long days in the fields, of suffering and sorrows, of joy and love. And when the time arrived for communion I stood up from my pew and followed them up the aisle toward the altar, where the priest presented me the body and blood of Christ as I stuck out my tongue and said, "Amen." I drank from the cup of Christ and ambled humbly back to my pew. Soon the mass ended. We walked out into the daylight to the sound of an organ.

Some of the children tugged on my pant legs, stared up

into my hollow, black eyes and smiled gentle smiles, laughing and dancing around, yelling out "Gringo," and asking for change. I picked up a small girl and held her above my head, moving in circles as she laughed gleefully in joyous delight. When I placed her back down all the others pulled on my shirt and begged for a ride. A hand clasped my right shoulder, and I turned around.

"Welcome brother," said the priest, "you must be new."

"Yes," I said, "I arrived last night."

"How did you enjoy the mass?"

"Very beautiful," I replied, "you are truly a man of God."

"Are you hungry?"

"Starving, but I must catch a bus."

"Come eat at my house, I'm eager to hear of your travels."

"I could use some food. I'm starving, to be honest."

"Look no further, you are welcome here."

We walked along a dirt path past ramshackle wooden huts, past gardens and fields, children playing in the streets, families gathered in the town park. We twisted our way back into the hillside, through mud and dung, over small rivulets and streams, past *fincas* of corn and yucca, till we finally arrived at the priest's modest concrete home situated up on a hill.

Some scrawny dogs greeted us at the doorway, begging for food. The priest threw them some stale bread and they attacked it voraciously as though it were prime rib. As we entered his home, I assessed the humble surroundings: a single mattress resting quietly in the corner, draped in mosquito netting, carefully swept concrete floors and unadorned concrete walls, a pale grey, the color of rain clouds. The kitchen boasted a small wooden table and a concrete counter. No appliances, no running water, and a single light bulb hanging from a cord dangling from the ceiling.

"Please, have a seat" he insisted.

So I sat.

"How do you take your coffee?"

"With milk," I responded.

"Just milk?" he asked. "Do you not enjoy the sweet things in life?"

"You mean sugar?"

"Yes sugar, but there are many other sweet things in life."

"Like love?"

"Love is perhaps the sweetest, but it must be the right kind of love."

"You mean like love for God?"

"Love for God, yes, but God is not distinct from other sweet things. He is in them all and lends his sweetness."

"I don't know if I understand," I remarked as he served me my cup of coffee and sat down in the chair beside me. The dogs ran through the kitchen and out the back door into the garden. A light breeze swept through the windows as the priest sipped his coffee and smiled, lines of wrinkles rippling along his forehead and from the creases of his deep blue eyes.

"Not many can understand, and even I, having devoted my life to his service can barely imagine the gravity of these words, but God is within everything, above everything, and yes, he is everything."

"So if I have forsaken a woman, a woman whom I love, have I then forsaken God?"

"Not if you truly love her. If there is love in your heart, nothing can disguise it. Love does not play games or hide behind masks."

"Then should I return and set things right?"

"That, my friend, only you can decide. All I can say is

135

that sometimes we end up where we did not intend and in finding our way back, we discover something of the divine, like a game of hide and seek in which we are both the hider and the seeker.

"I don't think I understand."

"This is the eternal game of divine seduction: We lose ourselves, then find ourselves; we are always hidden, yet always on our way to being found. To find your way you must look into your heart and decide whether you are the hider or the seeker."

"And if I am hiding from myself, how will I ever be found?"

"You must choose your path wisely, listen to your heart and heed no regard for the artful mind of reason; and when you finally discover your path, follow it to your final destination."

I sipped on my coffee and surveyed my surroundings, noting that there was not a single image of Christ anywhere in sight. The dogs came racing back through the kitchen as the priest tossed them some more bread. They tore it to pieces and devoured it.

"Truth is perhaps the greatest gift that God can give to man; discover your truth and you will find your path."

"I believe that truth can only be found in simplicity. It seems to me that you live a very truthful life."

"I am making my way, as we all are in this game. Now is the time for you to decide to quit and fold your hand, or to let the wind blow you onward toward your intended course."

"Yes, but I have no means at the moment. I have lost all my possessions and spent all my money. I'm on my way to Macas. Do you think you could loan me a few dollars?"

"It seems the fates shine in your favor. My nephew is on his way there this morning. I will arrange it so that you can ride with him."

"Thank you, sir. You have given me more than enough. How can I repay you?"

"I ask for nothing in return, only that you follow your fate and find your bliss."

* * *

As we passed through Puyo I noticed a distinct change, in both the people and the land. The sun was now high in the sky, bearing down on us with its burdensome rays. I hung tightly to the side of the truck as Manuel took the turns with heedless disregard. The road changed from broken asphalt to stone and sand. We were now in the Amazon Basin on the outskirts of the jungle where the vegetation was desiccated from want of rain. Skinny, malnourished cows ruminated on dry grass. I could tell we were no longer in the Andes, as the shape and character of the people morphed from the short, dark-skinned Incas of the Sierra to those with more angular countenances of a race, or perhaps many races, exemplified by the Indians of remote Amazon tribes eking out a livelihood in a modern society built on agriculture and trade as opposed to the hunter-gather life that had persisted for millennia. I held no qualms as we made our way south to Macas. My heart leaped with joy as we breeched on uncharted territory. I was fascinated by these people, these peasants donning rubber boots and mud-covered t-shirts, brandishing machete blades and bearing fruits and vegetables from the countryside. We stopped several times to converse with the locals and occasionally to pick up an extra body or two until the back of the truck was inundated with travelers. They spoke in foreign tongues that sounded like the dialect from my dreams of the jungle, an ancient sound unlike anything I knew. I traded glances with several of my fellow passengers, a nod or a smile, as I could tell they were intrigued by the presence of a disheveled gringo.

"Where are you heading?" asked a short, skinny man with a light complexion and long, dark hair.

"Macas," I answered.

"I live in Macas," he responded.

"Do you know a man named Emiliano Tséremp?" I inquired.

"Why do you ask?"

"He's a friend of mine. I'm going to be working with him."

"He's a friend of yours?"

"A friend of a friend."

"Yes, I know this man. Many men know this man."

"Do you know where he lives?"

"He is a very powerful man. I'm sure you will find him."

"Yes, but do you have an address?"

"Ask the locals, they will help you."

"Thank you," I uttered as he began to converse with his fellow travelers, motioned toward me with a look of intrigue and then grew silent.

The road turned to rubble as the truck banged from side to side. I held tight to my seat and admired the scenery. The scorched earth had become lush and verdant. Rolling hills of green encompassed the road, a narrow, broken path crossing over wide rampant rivers along thin metal bridges. I wasn't quite sure what to expect, from both the jungle and from the shaman. My dreams had led me to believe that I would be traveling by canoe into the depths of the forest to some remote outpost inhabited by ancient nomadic tribes. I imagined the man lean and angular, cut from stone, draped in the regalia of a priest-like figure; a crown of feathers, jewels of stone hanging from his neck. Of course I realized that my dreams were figments of my imagination and that reality doesn't always coincide with the apparitions inside our heads, but I sensed in the reverence of my fellow passengers that this man was of some importance and that I had not traveled in vain, that my dreams were not without some foundation.

By the time we arrived in Macas it was well into the afternoon and the sun was on its path over the Pacific. Manuel wished me luck outside the bus terminal in the heart of town. I thanked him for his charity and set my feet on the ground, adapting to my newfound surroundings: the busy streets, the noise of cars and buses, the burdensome heat. It felt like a unique blend of coast and sierra, more laid-back then Riobamba, but more urban then the fishing villages along the Pacific. The people were a mix of *mestizo* and Amazonian Indian, perhaps Shuar, perhaps Quichua. I had lost Emiliano's phone number along with the rest of my stuff, but from my conversation with the man on the truck I sensed it wouldn't be all that difficult to discover his whereabouts. I hailed a cab and asked in my best Spanish if he could take me to Emiliano Tséremp.

"Who?" he responded.

"Emiliano Tséremp, the shaman," I repeated.

"I don't know any shamans," he said. "You must mean the Shuar."

"Yes, the Shuar. Do you know this man?"

"There are many Shuar in Macas, but I don't know this man."

I continued on my way, making inquiries of local vendors and merchants without success, until a short, pleasant-looking Indian woman came up to me with a child perched on her shoulder.

"Would you like a woman?" she asked me.

"What?"

"A woman, would you like a woman?"

"No, I don't think so, I'm looking for a man of the Shuar

by the name Emiliano Tséremp. Do you know him?"

"Emiliano, yes I know him."

"Can you take me to him?"

"Ten dollars."

"I'm sorry, but I don't have any money."

"Oh," she hesitated, "then how' bout your watch?"

"So much for hospitality," I thought as I looked down at my watch and wondered if I even needed it, then looked back into her eyes and the face of the child resting against her neck.

"First get me Emiliano and then I will give you my watch."

She nodded in acquiescence and ducked into a local phone terminal to make a call. A minute or two later, she exited. "He will be here in about fifteen minutes. Now may I have my watch?"

"What did you tell him?"

"I told him a foolish white boy was waiting for him outside the bus terminal."

"And he understood who I was?"

"Yes, I think he understood."

I unhooked the black Casio from my left wrist and politely handed it over to the woman, keeping up my end of the deal, figuring she needed it more than I did at the moment. I smoked a cigarette as I waited for Emiliano with a somewhat restrained enthusiasm, excited and deeply curious, yet absolutely terrified at the prospect of working with the medicine in the depths of the jungle where tarantulas and boas would be waiting to attack; and of course there was always the chance of malaria or dysentery if the medicine didn't kill me first or drive me mad. But my curiosity, first awakened in Tena three years prior, had not let go of my imagination. I was emboldened by the books I had read and by the nightly visions excreted by my unconscious in the dark shades of night. Everyone I had met told me to reconsider. They told me I was mad, and I replied, "Then what's the difference?" But there was also something ordinary about the entire ordeal and I wasn't sure if the reality of the shaman and of the experience would match my expectations, which by now had become so grandiose that they hardly left room for improvement. Soon enough I was greeted by a large, intimidating Indian man wearing sandals and wide pants made of alpaca cloth, a tie-dyed t-shirt, his long, dark hair pulled back in a ponytail.

"Jack?" he asked. "Gabriela's friend."

"Yes," I submitted.

"You're two days late."

"There were some delays."

"Are you prepared?"

"As much as I will ever be."

"Where's your stuff?"

"It was stolen."

"Follow me; we will get something to eat."

I walked by his side up a few blocks and into a local café. We took a seat and he ordered us some food. Emiliano's dark, penetrating eyes fixed on me. I could only imagine what he must have thought, this disheveled white boy, lost and penniless, speaking bad Spanish.

"First you must know that you cannot eat anything sweet or salty or with too much fat. The medicine does not mix well with these types of food."

"I will try to do what you say."

"We will begin tonight to cleanse your body and spirit and you will take the medicine each night of your stay."

"Good."

"Do you have any experience?"

"Some."

"Ayahuasca is known as the purge. You will experience

chronic vomiting and diarrhea."

"I'm aware."

A pause.

"May I ask what your interest is?"

"In the medicine?"

"Yes."

"Just curious, I guess."

"This is just a novelty for you?"

"No, not entirely."

"Then what?"

"I'm sick with an affliction of the mind. I've been haunted by demons since I was young. I was told you know how to heal the sick and I'm asking for your help."

"I can only guide you. To heal yourself you must ask the medicine. Let it reveal your sickness, then learn from it."

"I'm anxious to begin."

"You must be prepared; you must be in a good frame of mind."

"Will we be trekking into the jungle this afternoon?"

"We will not be entering into the jungle; I have some land on the outskirts of town. I will give you a place to stay and provide you with meals. I have two doctors from Uruguay working with me; you will join them in the ceremony center for the next seven days."

The waitress laid our meals on the table with a look of reverence. Emiliano thanked her with a thoughtful nod as she scurried back to the kitchen. A few men came in from the street and greeted Emiliano in what I assumed was the Shuar language. They spoke respectfully in a serious manner, and I could tell this man was an important member of the community, both feared and revered, a true medicine man, a man who deals in magic. I ate my chicken in silence and listened intently to the conversation that I could not understand. The men shook my hand as they left, and

Emiliano ate his meal...

* * *

I awoke from a short nap on the dry-cracked earth of the ceremony center. A tall vine reached upward from the base of the altar, an orange mat of cloth laid with bottles and instruments, which I assumed would present themselves at the onset of our endeavor. The air was chill and the time was now nearing midnight. A small fire of red-hot embers was smoldering to ash in the center of the circular bamboo hut. I dragged my body up from my blanket, ambled outside and admired the heavens. The moon was nearly full and the stars shone brighter than I could ever recall, shifting moonlight, revealing the landscape of bamboo buildings spread across the compound. I entered a small wooden kitchen on the edge of the property and asked Emiliano's wife if there was any food available.

"Will you be taking the medicine tonight?" she inquired.

"Yes," I responded.

"You should fast; anything that goes down will soon come up."

"Oh."

My hunger was fierce, but perhaps I just had some butterflies in my gut in anticipation of the ordeal. I lit up a cigarette and walked about the property, admiring the view across the valley, a large river reflecting moonlight, thick forest consuming the landscape. There was something vaguely familiar about this place that I couldn't understand, but the whole thing felt absolutely right and I had no hesitation about taking the medicine. Emiliano soon emerged from one of the bamboo huts and gathered us into the ceremony center. Another Shuar man fed the fire with small kindling as one of the Uruguayan doctors knelt before the altar. He took hold of a large, green soda bottle and poured himself a shot of the liquid. Without hesitation and without consent he downed the shot and sat upon a bench circumscribing the interior of the hut.

"Are you ready?" asked Emiliano.

"Yes, ready."

"Would you like me to pour it for you?"

"Please."

I knelt down along the mat and psyched myself in preparation for ingesting the foul substance, praying that I wouldn't heave it up immediately and end my journey before it had even begun. Emiliano doled out a small dose of the thick concoction and handed me the tin. I looked down in disgust as its odious scent overwhelmed my senses. I held the tin to the sky, reconciled any remaining inhibitions, then choked it down as a violent shudder of repulsion sent waves of disgust throughout my body, the vile taste of rotting earth left lingering along my tongue and down my throat. I quickly drank some water and rested on my blanket as the medicine took action. Emiliano and the others took their turn as we sat in silence amongst the dim-lit shadows that danced across the walls, emanating from the embers of the fire.

Within minutes I felt my stomach groaning with distress. I was absolutely certain that I would soon vomit anything remaining in my gut, but with great will I kept it down, assured that it wouldn't take effect if I threw up too quickly. I began to feel mildly ill, somewhat dizzy and out of my senses. I held the brew down for another thirty minutes until my body was on the brink of eruption. I crossed the threshold and ran outside behind the fence along a precipitous slope leading down into the valley. I bent over and let go of the wretchedness churning inside me, vomiting in compulsive spasms.

I felt elated and relieved as the medicine took hold.

First, staring down at the river below with its yellow lights twinkling in the distance like fireflies in summer, I felt my heart beat faster and I began to worry that something had gone wrong, as though I might have been poisoned and on the verge of death. Then, as I closed my eyes, iridescent walls of bright, beaming light surrounded me with pulsing unseen energy. I was in awe! Wonderfully breathtaking, grandly pulsing light emerged from the background. I sensed an alien presence, and the voices of my youth came to comfort me. They welcomed me and said that they'd been waiting. It was then that I realized I had made contact with the plant spirit. The pyramids grew into alien dimensions and I was certain I had arrived. I wandered back into the ceremony center and curled up in a bed along the earth. Visions washed upon me, like waves of forgotten memories and hidden landscapes beneath the shadows of waking life. Graceful waterfalls cascaded down chasms into wide running rivers flowing through the land. Pulsing waves of energy flowed through the water like sweet drops of dew on a summer morning. I could touch and taste the visions, inhale them deeply. I felt awash with love. I could see lights from above, an aerial view of Manhattan, descending into the electric current running through each blinking light and shifting advertisement. I sensed the city as a grand motor consuming the earth's energy with each pulse of light; the people were afraid, disconnected and wary, like parts of a giant computer unconscious of its program. Upon opening my eyes the temple was quiet, except for the crackling of the fire and the electric hum of the chirping crickets. I glanced across the floor and saw beautiful Ana come to life out of the inert objects along the floor. She lay in bed, naked, hands clasped in prayer.

"Don't be afraid," she said, "there is only love."

"I didn't want to leave you," I answered.

"Then why did you leave?"

"Because you asked me to."

"Don't be afraid," she repeated, "there is only love, there is only love, there is only love..."

She continued to pray as my eyes remained transfixed on her lovely countenance until she faded into the dark and her angelic form transfigured back into the jungle, back to the mud, smoldering to ashes, dissolved into earth. I closed my eyes as the visions continued for the next hour until I slowly drifted off into reveries. The loud hum of the universe died down to an inaudible hiccup, the sacred had become the profane, the visions washed away, and I drifted off to bed in a deep and soundless slumber.

I awoke in the early dawn, wrapped in thick blankets, the air still chill. Unlike my experience in Montanita I didn't feel dizzy or sick, like the after-effects of consuming too much alcohol. Rather, I felt clear-headed and awake, as if a pristine snowfall enveloped my senses as a calm, vital energy pulsed through my veins. The other initiates were still asleep as I arose from the earth and stretched my legs. I squatted next to the fire, a few dying embers still emitting heat as the sun peeked out from the valley floor, a boundless stretch of emerald trees expanding in all directions.

Smoke was filtering out from the kitchen as I made my way across the compound to see if there was anything to eat. It felt as though I had excreted my entire being the night before. I felt empty and pure. Emiliano's wife, a middle-aged Shuar woman about five feet in height, with a round face and figure, was busy at the stove preparing a meal for the children. There were several young girls and boys gathered around the table, half-naked with filthy faces, potbellies and disheveled dark hair. None of them paid me much attention, and not even the wife acknowledged my presence.

"Good morning," I greeted them.

"Yes, good morning," she responded rather hastily. "How did you sleep?"

"Like a child," I told her, "The medicine was good."

She laughed loudly as she continued stirring a pot on the stove, "The medicine was good," she repeated, "the medicine was good...."

"It was the most beautiful vision."

"Yes, it can be beautiful, but you have much to learn."

"Is there anything to eat?"

"Yes, there is fruit. You must be careful what you eat."

"Yes, Emiliano told me."

"Nothing too sweet or salty and no fat."

"I will just have some fruit then."

I took some papaya and walked back outside. I was no longer cold as the sun rose in the sky. On the way back to my sleeping quarters I was greeted by a young, dark-skinned Shuar man with scars across his face.

"Would you like to see the vine?" he asked me.

"Yes."

"Follow me," he replied as we walked behind the kitchen and into the forest surrounding the compound. We traveled a short distance through the trees and bushes, until we came upon what appeared to be a thick rope wrapped in circles around a tree trunk about fifty feet high.

"This is ayahuasca," he said. "We grow some here, but we buy it by the kilo from some of our friends in the jungle. Today you'll be helping me prepare the brew. I'll show you what I know."

"Your name?"

"Javier. I'm Emiliano's nephew."

Back in the center of the compound, in about fifty yards of open dirt between the huts and the kitchen, we erected a tarpaulin ten feet tall like a small circus tent. Along the side of the ceremony center were situated about 200 kilos of the vine, held within plastic sacks. We dragged out a few sacks beneath the tent and unloaded them in a giant pile. We sat down upon some small logs and began sorting out the ayahuasca, a thick vine of dark brown about two inches in diameter, shaped like a double-helix. Javier handed me a knife and demonstrated the proper manner of shaving the vine. I practiced with my knife, cutting off the bark as Javier calmly instructed me and refined my method.

We continued like this for several hours as the aya-huasca piled high and the sun rose in the sky, revealing its merciless rays. I took refuge beneath the tent, but could not escape the wet heat of the Oriente. I was sweating profusely and eventually abandoned my shirt. By now the two Uruguayan doctors had awakened, joining us in preparing the brew while sipping from gourds of *yerba mate.*

"Try some," said the older one, an affable-looking man with a thick grey beard. I sipped from the gourd and was pleasantly surprised.

"Very good. Where did you get that?"

"We brought it from Uruguay. It's like coffee in America; we're very fond of our *mate.*"

"I'll have to look into that. What's your name?"

"Tomás, and this is my son," motioning to the younger one, "Andrés."

As we finished with the pile Javier showed me how to masticate the vine by pulverizing it with a hammer into twine-like sinew which would be used to prepare the brew. I understood from books I had read that the ayahuasca vine contains certain chemicals that, when prepared with a DMT-rich leaf from the jungle, create the psychedelic properties of the brew that render it orally active. DMT is a potent entheogenic substance found in the pineal gland of the human brain that has mystified and intrigued both scientists and psychonauts for at least a century.

When we had finished masticating the vine, Javier gathered it into two ten-gallon pots and brought them to the kitchen to be boiled with the leaf that he referred to as *yage.*

"This will take some time," he said.

Andrés, a light-skinned, heavy-set fellow of about twenty-four, offered to take me into town to check email and buy some supplies. I followed him past the fence, encircling the compound, out onto a muddy street that led us past some smaller bamboo houses with children playing outside and farmers carrying large machete blades. A bus picked us up at the intersection of two dirt roads, meandering its way into town, making stops and letting off passengers.

"Your name?" asked Andrés in heavily-accented English.

"You speak English?"

"A little."

"Jack."

"I've spent some time in the U.S., in Arizona, working with peyote."

"Mescaline."

"Yes."

"How does it compare to ayahuasca?"

"Peyote and ayahuasca are both good medicines, but very different."

"Yes, I had beautiful visions last night. I envisioned a girl I know come to life out of the earth. She was lying naked along her bed praying for me. I felt a deep, indescribable sense of love. I had never felt that way before."

"The medicine can only reveal what's inside of us, inside all of us. Ask your spirits to help guide your visions. With practice you will learn to find these feelings and say things without words."

"I didn't need words; words would have been useless."

Andrés laughed and patted me on the back as the bus came to a halt in front of a café. "You have a good head. You will learn much."

At an ATM outside of the national bank I checked my account and realized I had barely enough money to cover my expenses and make it back home. I withdrew several hundred dollars, carefully surveying my surroundings and stashing the bills it in my back pocket. Andrés and I visited a local internet café to check our email. Upon opening my inbox I discovered a message from Ana. A deep feeling of dread overcame me, and I could not summon the strength to open it, fearing that she would renounce my existence and banish me to a life of loneliness and despair. I also feared that any negative emotions could easily trickle into my psyche, corrupting my visions and impairing my work with the medicine.

Andrés finished up and we wandered the streets of Macas looking for a bite to eat and a shop where we could purchase some supplies. We stopped at a local café and ordered lunch. As we waited a young Shuar man with an angular face and black hair greeted us in Spanish.

"Are you the American working with Emiliano?" He posed his question in my direction.

"Yes, how did you know that?"

"What I know is beside the point. The real question is why you are working with him?"

"I don't know what you mean."

"Emiliano does not have the best intentions. Emiliano deals in black magic. You would do best to come with me."

"What do you mean, he deals in black magic?"

"Emiliano is a socerer, very powerful and very dark. If you continue under his guidance you will be lost, and not even I can bring you back."

"How do I know you're telling the truth?"

"Listen to your visions and let them guide you. You have been warned once. This may be your last warning."

At just that moment a dark cloud covered the sun, possibly a sign portending dark things to come. A large figure appeared at the door. As he entered, the small Shuar man humbly, eyes on the floor, shuffled outside. They exchanged a glance and a few heated words, then the figure became clear. Emiliano in a deeply sullen manner sat down at our table.

Andrés greeted Emiliano warmly and excused himself from the table, leaving us alone and silent.

"How was the medicine last night?"

"You mean aside from all the vomiting and shitting?"

"How were your visions?"

"Breathtaking, more beautiful than anything I've ever seen."

"For the medicine to heal you, it is necessary to purge the body. You must vomit and shit if you want to work on the spirit."

"I understand."

"And what did you see?"

"I saw an alien universe, large cities made of light. Beautiful landscapes, rivers and oceans, mountains and deserts. I saw Manhattan from above and felt a deep sense of fear. Then my girlfriend praying naked alongside her bed. I felt loved, deeply loved."

"The medicine is welcoming you; you've taken to it well. Try not to eat much today. Fasting is part of the shamanic ordeal. Tonight I must go to Quito on business. You will take the medicine again with the doctors. Listen to the voices, let them guide you. The medicine purges not only the body, but the psyche as well. You must learn to let go of your fears, anxieties, and regrets. Only then may you ascend to the next level."

"I understand."

"Before I go, do you have the money?"

"Gabriela said seventy dollars a day."

"I told her eighty."

"I have five hundred dollars, the last of my money."

Emiliano looked upset, pensive for a moment as he stared into the distance.

"Because you are friends with Gabriela I will make an exception. But you must be willing to stay till the end of the week."

"Of course."

"And you must do as I say."

"Yes, yes, of course."

"That means avoiding contact with frauds like the one who just left."

"He said you're a sorcerer. What did he mean by that?"

"He meant nothing. He's a fraud, a trickster looking for a client. You must remain vigilant in town; avoid unsavory characters and women offering you a good time. You must refrain from sex and keep to your fasting."

"I will do as you say."

"I have some things to take care of. You can take the bus and meet the others back at the compound. Try to rest and prepare yourself for this evening."

I handed him the money from my back pocket, and he politely excused himself from the table. I quietly finished my meal, drank a cup of juice, and headed back out into the daylight, the strong sun glaring down with its relentless rays.

* * *

I boarded the wrong bus and took an unnecessary detour on my way back to the compound. Everything looked the same to me: the same bamboo huts, the same dirt gravel roads, the same fields and forests. After a few hours of heading in the wrong direction I found an intersection that seemed familiar. The bus driver let me off and I wandered some dirt roads till I found the compound. Tomás and Andrés were busy beneath the tarp, preparing ayahuasca under Javier's direction. The brew we had prepared this morning was nearly finished, boiling down to the thick, awful concoction that I had become familiar with. I joined the men in masticating the vine, listening to their conversations, of which I understood little.

"What does the medicine teach you?" I asked Javier.

"It teaches me how to prepare the medicine."

"Are you practicing to become a shaman like your

uncle?"

"I'm not a shaman's apprentice, if that's what you are asking. Shamans must be called upon, mainly by sickness or dreams. I am here to prepare the medicine. This is my job."

"What do you mean 'called upon?'"

"A young shaman is given a sign, either by spirits or by our ancestors. Sometimes he is ill, sometimes mad. Through his hallucinations or by the will of dreams he is summoned into the vocation of shaman. He must go through many ordeals, dismemberment, solitude, and fasting for days on end. Through his healing he gains power and wisdom, only then may he seek the path of the shaman."

"Is Emiliano a good shaman?"

"Emiliano is one of the best."

"Are his intentions always good?"

"Emiliano is a true healer. He does what is necessary to cure his patients."

We continued working with the ayahuasca till the day grew old and the sun sank low. My thoughts at this time of day were entirely with Ana, of how my departure might have upset her, of how she might be suffering because of my reckless abandonment of what might have been a fulfilling relationship. But last night when she visited me in my visions, I felt sure that she was with me--if not physically, then mentally or spiritually. I sensed that despite our separation, our bond was as strong as ever. My thoughts were of her as her prayers were of me. Love does not play games or hide behind masks. I wanted to ask her for forgiveness. I wanted to make amends and profess my love, but I knew I needed more time with the medicine.

Midnight was fast approaching when Emiliano left for Quito. Prior to his departure he warned me not to allow the dogs into the ceremony center. However, soon after he left I could not resist their affectionate yelps and let them in to cozy up near the fire. We soon commenced our ritual, doling out the medicine and quickly choking it down, each of us shuddering in his own way, taking our places about the hut.

Again I was able to hold the medicine down for about thirty minutes when I noticed the need to purge. I quickly ran outside behind the fence and let it all out, vomiting and shitting until I was cleansed. As I quietly walked back toward the fire, I took notice of the San Pedro plants glowing in a ghostly green. They were bending and writhing beneath the moonlight like alien life forms from a parallel universe. One particular San Pedro plant asked of my intentions.

"Do you wish to eat me?" it inquired.

"I don't know," I responded.

"Be not afraid," he replied, "we were bred from a different earth, one that has not learned of things such as hatred, hell, and despair."

Just then I noticed a cat creeping from the cacti, and I fled in fright back to the ceremony center. I shut my eyes and was overwhelmed by the dark, the dark that ran so deep it appeared as nothing, nothing more than being itself. I was attached to nothing, from thought or form. It was a lonely place, but I felt safe and secure. I lay there for awhile, not thinking or breathing, heart beating still, the world still silent. Then I was overwhelmed by the sense that I was back in the womb, submerged in embryonic fluid, warm and content. This was also the feeling of floating in a deep dark space, a void of nothing, a void non-being or yet to be. The one sensation that I was aware of was the beating of my mother's heart, a beat so strong that it fed me without fear. It told me of what was to come and pacified my fears with the promise that her affectionate caress would not let me go, not until I was ready to fly on my own. Then there was incoherent babble, a loud prattle of dissonant sounds, and the appearance of a harsh and unexpected light pulling me downward.

"I'm afraid!" I wanted to shout.

But my mother's heart spoke to me, "It will be alright my son," it said, "I will be waiting."

Comforted by this promise, unspoken and without sound, I let go of my worries and let the light pull me down. Then, just as I began to emerge from the dark, from the deep dark space, barren and alone, I entered the pulsing electric grid of all humanity, like an electron through a circuit, shot through time and space, only to enter the vast cave of human history.

There was the soft hum of a sitar playing from somewhere deep in the cave, and I was first confronted by yogis deep in meditation, humming their mantras internally, radiating love and eternal bliss. Then came priests and rabbis reciting prayers and bowing to their Gods, followed by large Buddhas, soft and content, casting off the shackles of material reality, the rusting façade of human endeavors, only to unite with the collective consciousness of all reality. Then there were shamans, dancing and singing around fires reaching towards the heavens. They were dismembered, tortured, transported through the vast abyss of heaven and earth, only to be put back together, having traveled through the devil's den to emerge with secret knowledge, having passed through the trials of all the ages, to be reborn, to come back as healers. And there were kings and queens, and leaders of all nations, wearing flowing robes and crowns made of jewels and gold. They were all communing as one, as one heart beating loud and strong like that of my mother's in the deep space of the womb, reassuring humanity that there is more than earth and sky, forest and ocean. Underneath the vast layers of illusion the world sparkled with a wonder that could not be expressed in words or sound, but solely through the experience, solely through the endeavor of communion.

And it was then that I heard the loud beat, the loud techno-beat of the modern world. A large stage emerged within the cave, as the holymen faded to black, and lights came from the sky; red, blue and yellow, they came whirling around to the sound of the loud and deafening beat. Models came parading down the stage, wearing scant clothing, cloaked in ego-seeking satisfaction, intoxicated by self-importance. They strut up and down as the lights blinked to the beat, and the onlookers sitting behind their screens reached out to an ensemble of idols, both out of admiration and envy, of lust and worship. This was the new era, the era of the self. The old gods had died and new gods had emerged. We now became our own gods, the center of all the cosmos, the star in the sky around which the universe revolved. And here I was, a young child born to this world, and I was to become my own star, gathering the universe in my hand through the laws of attraction, through the physical laws of gravity, I was to become my own maker, my own idol, my own force of nature. I would surround myself with the idea that I was of the greatest importance, whether through the love and hate of my onlookers, whether through their admiration or contempt. I would become more important than all the men and women of all the ages, I would be the savior of all that was good and right, I would shine magnificently beneath my cloak of beauty, invoking wonder in my onlookers, intriguing them through my charisma and magnetic charm, through my devout contentment and keen mind. And they would admire me in all my glowing radiance, and they would talk night and day, day and night about my loveliness, about the virtue of my character and the perfection of my ideals. But these voices would rot inside my head, they would turn deathly sick and speak ill of my triumphant heart. The despair of the darkest ocean would fill me with fault. As they once admired me they would now shout "bloody hell!" and march over my ego, trampling my sensitive nature with the hardened soles of their feet, with the stubbornness of their hearts. And I would be left alone, I would be left to the darkness, to the abyss, the bottom chasm of the deepest ocean where nothing could save me, where nothing could touch me, where nothing could let me feel the touch of my mother's heart that promised it would never let go, not let go until I was ready to depart on my own.

And then came a voice, soft and somber: "Get better my child," it whispered, "always have faith and you will never know despair, always have hope and you will never know darkness."

And then they shut the coffin and piled the earth high and I was left to the voices, the thousands of voices of all the earth, speaking ill and speaking praise, flattery and malicious scorn, of my imminent downfall and of all that could have been, but never came to flower. And then, distinct from all things, separate from the cacophony of this loud, contemptible, incoherent rant, came the last thing I would remember, the only voice that ever mattered, the last bastion of truth where there appeared to be none. "Know one thing," it said. "Know one thing and you can find a way out."

And there in the darkest shadows of the sylvan green stood a young Indian child holding out her hand. "Come with me," she said. "Now that I've found you you'll never be lost again." And so I gently reached out from my own disillusionment and grasped the young girl's slender fingers. "How did you find me?" I asked. "I just listened to my heart," she told me. "It's time you listened to yours."

We emerged from dense jungle growth that encompassed us on all sides into the bright encampment of our tribe, men and women, young and old, child and mother, father and son singing soulfully around the fire dancing up the heavens.   They welcomed me back from my travels, referring to me as their "warrior of the light," offered me a gourd of *chicha* and a spot at the fire.   And then the stars fell apart, the cosmos stopped spinning, the planets ceased their rotation, and I was caught in the moment, not yearning or seeking, not wishing or hoping or regretting or fearing.   I had arrived, with my daughter at my side.

I awoke to the sound of shuffling feet, only to open my eyes and notice Emiliano's niece exiting from the ceremony center. I quietly lifted myself from the earthen floor and began to pack my bags. My visions from the night before were still fresh in my mind and I came to the conclusion that I had learned what I came for. All I needed now was to reconcile with Ana, plead at her feet that she acknowledge the error of my ways and take me back in her arms. As I was packing, Emiliano arrived at the gate.

"What is this about?" he questioned me. "You have a long way to go."

"You can keep your money, Emiliano. I've found what I needed."

"You made a pact to stay till the end of the week. If you leave now there's no telling what might happen to your mind. You are not yet healed."

"Sometimes pacts are meant to be broken, and sometimes pacts are meant to be reconciled."

Then he stood tall, towering and ominous in a way, like he had appeared back at the café. "Listen to me now, as though your life depended on it. Whatever you experienced last night, no matter how profound, was only a piece of the puzzle, a fragment of an ever-coalescing whole that has yet to become solid. These are the fragments of your psyche and you risk falling back into madness if you do not continue."

I stood silent for a moment and pondered these words. I recalled my error in leaving Ana too soon and how it had damaged me. Perhaps, I thought, if I leave too soon, once more I will suffer even greater consequences. "But what does my heart tell me?" I asked myself. "What does the one, unchallenged voice have to say?" My heart stayed silent, so I quietly submitted and agreed to Emiliano's terms.

"Good," he replied, "Today we trek into the jungle to take ayahuasca beneath the falls. Gather your things and prepare yourself."

Then he turned and headed back to his hut, as I unpacked my bags and submissively wandered to the kitchen. By the time I had finished breakfast the doctors had awakened. Andrés greeted me in English, and I asked him if we could head into town so I could resolve some issues.

"What issues?" he asked

"I need to hear from a dear loved one," I told him.

We quickly headed out the gate, heading toward the corner where our bus would pick us up and bring us to town. Although I may have committed to carrying through with the ordeal, I needed to hear from Ana, to hope that all was not lost."

We walked the streets of Macas under the scorching sun until we made our way to the internet café where my fate awaited me. Whether to fall from the tallest tree or to be saved by the softest hand? I sat down at the computer and opened my email account. Amongst the multitude of junk mail and a few messages from friends and family back home, there it stood: a single note from Ana that would shatter my heart or lift me from the abyss into everlasting bliss. And with the click of a mouse the truth revealed itself:

Dear Jack,

Since the night you left my heart has been in all kinds of chaotic flux. Until that night I had never been drunk and when I awoke the following morning at dawn, in our bed alone and silent, I began to recall just what had happened. I could not fathom the outcome of my actions. That woman, that woman dancing with that man was not the woman you know, but a troubled creature yearning for affection, a confused creature intoxicated and out of her senses. Jealousy, too, had taken hold and that kiss and its aftermath was simply a slip of the tongue. I kissed the wrong man, and now the man that I love is long gone.

Once more my dreams spoke to me. I dreamt the two of us were seated by ourselves in an empty café, a single flame flickering between us, holding hands across the table, tears melting down our faces and collecting into puddles along the tablecloth. I asked you why you had left and you responded, "Because you asked me to." Then I recalled the sad song, the boiling blood, the heated thrashing of fists and broken flesh. And then, yes, I had screamed with all my breath for you to leave, to leave and "never come back." I now regret those naïve words, those words that only wish they had the wisdom to hold you tight before you departed.

But we humans are not a perfect breed. We are infinite in our actions and everlasting in our deeds, but we act out of our own imperfections, only hoping to one day reach our ideals, to endure pain and misery through the trials of all the ages, only to burn off the stubborn burden of our own inadequacy and commune with the heavens. We are creatures of habit looking to change, we creatures imbued with purpose, finding our way. And one day, we will look back on a lifetime of struggles and know just which path to follow, which road to tread.

As I once said, "Love isn't about yearning, it's about being a part of something bigger than yourself." When man loves man, and when man loves nature, and when man loves God, we all work together. Through our deeds and through the tales told by our tongues, we all dance at once, we all breathe the same breath and our stubborn hearts all beat in unison, not out of yearning, but out of communion. And when we share this experience we pass it on to the youth, so that out of the misery of our existence a new age is born, a new age travels a different path, a new age reaches for the heavens, knowing that they will never fade, knowing that if they just stand tall, the world will forgive their follies. If they just have faith, the world will go on living.

And if the world can forgive man then perhaps we can forgive each other, perhaps upon the moment of our departure we still traveled same path, we were still reaching out for the same hand. Some things take longer than forever, and sometimes we must just keep on waiting, but I have come to know one thing: patience is the one true virtue, wait long enough and the world will come to you. And when you knock on my door at the end of eternity and I'm old and wrinkled like a prune, you will smile that silly smile and once again we will grow young, the layers of illusion will shed their false façade and as you stare in my eyes, as you seep through my pores and beat with my heart we will find our sanctuary, we will find our one thing, and we will no longer be lost.

Te Amo por Siempre,
Ana

As a single tear drop formed in the corner of my eye and fell gently from my face onto my chest, I looked down at the necklace hanging from my neck and there, carved out of stone, was the image of a scorpion, the image of a partnership forged under the foaming mouth of *Pailon*, the image of Ana holding out her hand. I wanted to leap from my chair and run a thousand miles if just for a kiss, but I was certain that patience is the one true virtue and if we could just wait long enough the world would coincide with our ideals, and our paths would unfold toward the same destination. So, I did the only thing I could do and wrote a response:

Dear Ana,

For me to corrupt the only thing I ever loved is an act more violent than any fist could conjure, and for me to cause you to awake alone and sick, to awake with regret and aching sorrow is an act more shallow than that of the most perverted narcissist. As you trudged back to our hotel, intoxicated and out of your senses, I rode through the dark, I rode through the night on my way to the realization that this was not the journey I had planned, this was not the path I intended. But before I ever met you I was at a crossroads in my life, I stood outside a bus terminal smoking a cigarette and without knowing, out of my own ignorance and folly I had missed my intended ride only to arrive at my destination at the wrong point in time. But sometimes the universe conspires in our favor and what seemed to be the wrong point in time was a sign portending fate, revealing the will of our destiny, shedding the face of eternity and letting the naked breast of the world seductively compel us to reach through the grim exterior and find the soft flesh beneath, to find our intended path and realize our purpose. And because of that mistake, and because of an infinite amount of mistakes before we met, I noticed you surreptitiously sneaking glances from beneath your computer screen and found the will and fortitude to offer you a smile.

And when we spoke I understood that we had met an infinite amount of times before that event, before my mistake and the thousands of mistakes that led me to you. And I knew from that moment I never wanted to depart, that I never wanted to ride another bus without you by my side. Then, erroneously lost in my own ignorance and intoxicated by my own lust and envy I made another mistake and left too early, I departed clandestinely beneath the shade of a waxing moon, and the creatures of the night mocked me for my ignorance, mocked me for my own bad habit.

That night, under the spell of ayahuasca, I envisioned your coming to life out of the inanimate objects forming my surroundings; lying naked along your bed, hair softly caressing your neck, your hands were held in prayer and you repeated the same line again and again: "There is only love, there is only love, there is only love..." And because of your prayer I no longer feared the dark, I no longer feared the unknown hiding in the farthest corners of my mind. And then I learned that fear is the root of all neuroses, that because of fear I have squandered my life and fed it to the hounds of madness, to the beasts of insanity. The dread that I once knew, the voices that once consumed my own psyche, devouring every last scrap of what I knew to be truth, became one, not a thousand incoherent rambling strangers, but one voice soft and clear, the voice of a young girl holding out her hand.

We were lost, lost for ages--and now that I've found you again I will fight with all my will not to let you go, not to let you trudge through eternity frightened and alone. I recall those first moments of our encounter, the soft contours of your lips, the nervous tremble of your fingertips, the hollow light radiating from within, and now that I envision your smile, I cannot let go, I cannot bear the thought that we will ever be alone. When I return, after the final night of ceremony, with the wisdom endowed by a more profound form of knowledge, I will not shed tears for having left my former life behind, I will simply stand in front of your gentle eyes and radiant smile, and I will gently caress your shoulder and promise never to leave again.

Love,

Jack

As I finished my response and sent it to Ana I was certain of my intended path. Although I knew that my plane would depart in one week's time, nothing would keep us apart, no matter what distance, no matter what grievance. Andrés and I soon finished up our business at the internet café and made our way through town back to the bus stop. I noticed something peculiar as we ambled down the streets, something in the faces of the villagers seemed different or changed, as though they recognized me as a familiar acquaintance. Odd glances, sly smiles, the eyes of strangers snickering behind my back. It was as though they all knew me intimately, as though they could read my thoughts through some force of mental telepathy. For the moment I ignored this peculiar quirk in the fabric of reality as we made our way back to the compound to ready ourselves for our trek into the jungle.

Back at the ceremony center we packed our bags and prepared ourselves for the long hike to the falls. The time was now nearing noon and the sun was bearing down with its merciless rays. The heat became intolerable and for lack of food and lack of sleep my body grew weary, sweating profusely and ready for sleep. Emiliano announced that it was time to depart and we all gathered ourselves and our stuff in the back of his nephew's truck. Along the way, over rampant rivers and uneven rocky roads, we witnessed farmers trekking back from the fields, covered in muddy attire, the blades of their machetes hanging by their sides or over their shoulders. Women were washing clothes behind their bamboo houses as children came back from school dressed in charcoal grey slacks and dresses. The world continued as it always had, and although the faint sense of the villagers' recognition had passed, I felt somewhat connected to the people of this land. An unfamiliar landscape, an exotic place and time had soon become familiar, as though I had after years of travel, after many years of sailing around the sea, only to come back home and rest my weary bones.

Soon enough we arrived at the trail that reached back through farms and fields into the jungle. We emptied out of the truck, gathered our stuff and began our march. The sun blazed, and our weary feet felt heavy against the earth. Sweat consumed us and the heat was burdensome, but the reward awaiting us deep in the sylvan green was enough to keep us moving, to keep us plodding footstep by footstep. Along the way, we came upon a hut with earth floors. Emiliano engaged a fellow Shuar in their common tongue, reminding me of the shaman in my dreams. They offered us *chicha* as they continued conversing, at first in a serious, formal manner, then soon lighthearted and jovial. They laughed heartily and we were soon on our way. I asked Emiliano just what had taken place and he mentioned a dispute over these lands, but the owner was willing to let us pass when the quarrel was resolved.

We trekked along muddy paths through wetlands and then desiccated fields where skinny, malnourished cows fed on straws of hay, their forms hidden within bushes for want of shade. We continued for hours, stopping often to rest and rejuvenate ourselves with water and fruit. We continued on into the all-consuming forest, a verdant monster that encompassed us on all sides, dense organic matter reaching up from the ground and into the sky, the fragrance of fruit and earth overwhelming our senses, the calls of birds and the howls of monkeys off in the distance. At one point we were confronted with a raging stream and were compelled to cross along a fallen log, thin and slippery. We each made the crossing with care and vigilance. Soon enough, we had reached the other side, only to march another mile or so to arrive at our destination. The falls could be heard in the distance, and when we had reached a small clearing of grass where we would camp for the night, I caught my first glimpse of the gushing water rushing over the cliffside and gathering in a small pool of pristine water.

We set up our beds underneath a large plastic tarp as the night took over. An orange-pink hue off on the horizon seeped through the forest until all was dark. The moon peeked out, nearly full, and soon enough the stars began to shine radiantly, more numerous and more brilliant than I had ever seen, not even in the deserts of Mexico, not even in the prairies of the American Midwest. And as they shone, I recalled my first conversation with Ana, about the silence between words, like the dark between stars. I realized that the silence had ended as the stars patched together so nearly that all that remained was radiance, and the distance between us was no longer silent.

We constructed a fire encircled by stones, and Emiliano gave the word that our ceremony was about to begin. We inhaled tobacco juice up our noses and bathed ourselves in cologne as Emiliano rolled a thick cigar of tobacco and blew smoke up and down the length of our bodies. With palm fronds he waved the smoke, continuing to exhale until we had all been cleansed. He uttered solemn words and poured out the medicine. As in Montanita I had prepared to excrete my entire being. I had made certain to have sufficient toilet paper and had dug a small pit away from camp out in the bush. One by one we imbibed the foul substance of rotting compost, then silently awaited for the moment, the moment when we would purge, only to rest silently on our mattresses and allow the visions to overwhelm us.

As I waited, with some trepidation as I have always been averse to vomiting, I lay along the earth, my head atop a weathered rock, and admired the heavens. I began to imagine the patterns as symbols from throughout history, woven together like the star of David and the cross of Christ. I saw images of Islam, the ying and yang of Taoism, large Buddhas in quiet repose, wise old yogis deep in meditation. Then, without forewarning, the moment arrived. My guts emptied deep from the ducts until there was nothing left within, nothing but pure, pristine energy, the sacred descending from above, enveloping my senses and calming any hesitation.

I lay upon my mattress, my head cradled by the soft contours of my pillow, my body wrapped in an alpaca blanket. I slowly closed my eyes as the visions took hold and my journey into the unknown had begun. As before, I could hear the loud hum, the "wa-wa-wa" sound composing the grand motor of ourselves and of the universe. The ground began to quake and swallow me whole. I was immersed in the trenches of earth, snakes slithering from within the compost, insects burying me alive, devouring my flesh, gnawing on my bones. I was horrified by the unexpected turn of my trip, but realizing that fear feeds fear I let the frenzy continue, I let the most vile and loathsome creatures of the earth devour my body, feast on the entrails of my rotting corpse. And I was eaten whole till even my bones turned fodder, till my corpse had transfigured back into soil. Then I passed deep below the earth, beneath the soil, beneath the bedrock, down into the fiery chasms of hell only to be tortured, dismembered, and thrown into the deep pits of fire and fury. I burned for what seemed an eternity, where bodies were bought and sold at market, rotting flesh reeking with a repulsive odor, the scent of death stagnating like the smell of burning sulfuric acid. There were races from all humanity, all the tribes feasting on human entrails, bile spilling out and dripping down demonic faces, wild contorted features, half man, half beast. Blood boiled, the earth soaked with it, death and decay consumed my senses as the beasts danced and chanted around burning trenches of shit and entrails, conjuring sickness, burning with pain and anguish, the sharp, bloody edges of obsidian axes hacking through bodies, dismembering and devouring rotting appendages. And as this demonic gorging fest instilled terror in my heart, I turned to my side and puked the churning rancid remains of whatever shit was left inside me. I puked and then ran to the bush to shit, to excrete my entire body, my entire being till I was pure and pristine like mountain water running off into chasms.

And as I shit I noticed Emiliano lost in trance working through me. I recalled the shaman from the café and was overcome by anxiety. The fear of black magic consumed me and paranoia seeped into my consciousness; worry piled on worry as the trip continued. Lying back down along my mattress, I closed my eyes, focusing all my energy on Ana and that gentle little girl holding out her hand. But lost in the belly of the beast, love was not enough, faith played little part, the ugly faces of gorging demons sought nothing but to satiate their voracious appetite for decay and ruin. Lucifer himself reigned over this world, like the deathly shadow of a war not won, a war between good and evil, a battle fought in the trenches of the deep, in the chasms of hell.

Lost in this bizarre, sick, perverted battle, this gruesome, raging war of composting entrails, I thought of only one thing, one thing that might save me, one thing that might redeem me, and as in my dreams just one week ago, I listened to that silly voice and just let go. I let the beasts consume me. I let the howls and yips of blood-thirsty wolves descend from the sky and tear at me. And as I burned, and as the excruciating pain of torture and dismemberment continued, I ascended a ladder up the chasm walls, I ascended like evaporated water up into the clouds. Large pillowy masses of moisture, big white cotton balls of water gathered in the heavens as angelic faces appeared from nothing, like apparitions emerging at dawn. Beautiful women of all the races beckoned from pristine, untouched shores of deserted islands, seducing me with their artful glances, the soft contours of their pouty lips, the curvaceous flesh of their milky white breasts. A saintly chorus of sweet, nubile women rang in the empty hollows of this vast empty universe, all singing out, all luring me, all caressing my body with their soft brown skin, the lovely scent of their long, flowing hair. I was overwhelmed by lust, by the deep attraction of the saintly virgins, ensnaring me, willing me to let down my guard and make love for the remainder of time. Then, beneath the skin of appearances rose the face of an angel soft and clear. She held my gaze and lured me inward till her arms wrapped around my shoulders and down my back, till I sensed something amiss, something distinctly unfamiliar, like the writhing of a serpent, whispering in my ear. And just as we were about to make love came the slither of a sharp and biting tongue, "Now I will bear your fruit and the world will go on."

And although I yearned to be with her, and although every fiber within me wished to consummate our love, I felt the grip of death himself, the deceit of a sly trickster seducing me into a life of toil and pain, of hardship and struggle outside the Garden of Eden, alone and barren. I quickly seized the throat of the beguiling serpent while he was still intent on consuming my flesh. I pulled my sword from its scabbard and pierced him in the belly. With a loud wail he took the blow, then continued to wrap the girth of his leathery body about my waist, attempting to wrench the life from my breast. And as he overcame me, as I struggled to regain my sanity, I reached out with all my strength as he came lunging at my groin, sharp fangs filled with poison ripping through the soft flesh and penetrating what remained of my contorted body. The poison seeped into my veins, ran its course, pumping into my heart, leaving me weary with the sickly taste of death. I struggled to remain on my feet, to prevent the evil of this malicious beast strangle and consume me. With one last ounce of strength I grabbed for my blade, held it high and beheaded the foul creature speaking madness in my ear. I remained vigilant as his body let go and slunk to the floor, back down to the fiery depths of hell, hissing and moaning, the echo of his venomous tongue dying in the deep. I was no longer up in the heavens as the chorus of virgins faded in the distance, but lying in bed with Ana, my head upon her chest.

"Something the matter, my dear?" she asked.

"A bad dream, I guess. Recollections from a bygone era."

"A memory from your past?"

"The dread of youth, fanciful apparitions from a time long gone."

A moment of silence held our words at bay, as she kissed me and continued to caress my hair.

"Were we ever young?" she asked. "I can't recall. It seems like a dream, like the faint memory of a former life. We were children once, I remember that. I remember my father taking me to the park to watch the llamas graze, to paddle boats about the pond, to picnic amongst the weeping willows. Then one day I met you, and we kissed along the riverside, and I knew with all my heart that you would be here with me, to lie in bed and grow old in the great autumn of life."

"Yes, I recall quite clearly that vision of your unchallenged beauty. I knew it would never fade. Though my memory may come and go, that moment left a scar on my heart. I was always aware that we shared a deep history, that sometime long ago you had lost me or I had lost you. Then we met and

I kissed you. At that moment I knew I would not die alone, rather we would die together, both the predator and her prey."

"And how will I die if you don't eat me?"

"Then I will eat you!" I exclaimed, as I kissed her along the forehead.

"How silly are men," she said, "thinking they are a lion, when all they are is a shriveled-up turtle."

"And on our back rests the world."

The lights dimmed, a smug grin on my face as I opened my eyes and peered at the heavens, the tangled armies marching in the sky, Emiliano seated by the fire, the cold air, the muted sounds of animals lurking about the jungle floor. And as the medicine released its hold, as I regained my faculties and sense of reality, a long line of ants marched in the night, carrying leaf scraps back to their hole, quietly and patiently turning like cogs, and I turned as well, not yearning or seeking, but with a firm understanding that I was not alone.

At dawn, as the sun seeped through the tangled growth, shedding soft streaks of light across my pillow, I awoke with a deep pain in my abdomen and what seemed to be an enlarged left testicle. I recalled my vision from the night before, of the foul beast and his venomous bite, and then I thought twice and remembered my final night with Ana and how I had departed before my final injection.

Emiliano was awake and seemed to have been awake for some time. As we each arose from our beds, he handed us drinks and gathered us around the fire. I stood up with some hesitation, burdened by the pain, each step forward more challenging than the one before. And once we were all standing tall, his words grew solemn. Tonight we would begin the ceremony of *Natemamu*, a Shuar word meaning to die and be reborn. The ceremony would take place back at the compound, where at the moment of sundown we would begin to ingest *natem*, an ayahuasca tea prepared without *yage*. We would drink it from gourds and we would vomit without ceasing, but we would be compelled to continue with the will and fortitude of a warrior facing down his enemy in the heat of battle.

This endeavor intrigued me, as this is what I had come for, to die to the past and embrace the future, a new man healed of his scars, ready for a new life. But I had faced the greatest battle the night before, had slain my demon and avoided temptation, only to lie in bed with the only woman who ever mattered. And with the pain in my groin growing with each moment I stood, I asked Emiliano for a word alone.

"I know," he said.

"You know what?" I asked.

"I know you have been poisoned and I know you must leave."

"And the pact?"

"Some pacts are meant to be broken and some pacts are meant to be reconciled."

"Thank you, Emiliano, you are a kind man and a great healer. There is much for me to learn, both from you and from myself."

"You asked the medicine and the medicine gave you an answer. This was not the answer you were looking for, but the one you needed. All that I ask is that you continue with your fast and refrain from sex for the next ten days. Your mind is well, I have seen it for myself, but you risk losing everything if you do not obey."

"I understand," I said. "Maybe I have been healed or maybe I have been saved, but I have come to understand one thing and now I will no longer be lost."

He patted me on the shoulder and we gathered ourselves back around the fire. Andrés and Tomás would continue on with *Natemamu*, while I would depart on the next bus, unsure of the outcome, but with the unchallenged conviction that I must go on.

We marched towards the falls as I held tight to my abdomen, each step a painful contraction, each step closer to my destination. We wound through vines and bush, trees reaching for the sky, a maze of vegetation brimming with life and pulsing with energy. The falls crashed down from the tall cliffs above. We stripped naked and immersed ourselves in frigid jungle waters. And as the water flowed over me, I became more and more aware that I was awake, that I was alive. As my body was consumed by its icy clutch, I realized that my greatest adventure still awaited me.

We screamed with pain, we wailed with joy, shouted in a language unknown to this earth. Each step closer to the falls, was closer to a new life, I had died and now I was born, and when I arrived I would ask Ana to be my wife.

The bus pulled up to the station at noon, as Emiliano's truck receded in the distance. I finished the last drag off of my cigarette and considered quitting, extinguished the smoke with my foot and took my seat toward the back. We traveled on rocky roads of sand and stone, men and women frequently boarding, all with smiles, commendable cheer and joy in their humble, weather-beaten faces. If ants smile like that, I thought, then maybe being an ant isn't all that bad.

The day wore on as we meandered out of Puyo and up into the mountains. Valleys so vast and mountains so tall it stretched the imagination. *The sun began to descend as the Shuar lined up along a bench on the edge of the compound. Night was unfolding, each of the doctors holding hollowed-out shells filled with natem.* My body was in pain, but my heart could not contain the joy of what awaited me just a few hours down the road. Vendors boarded at small mountain villages, selling chicken and rice, boiled yucca, and tamales wrapped in cornhusks.

The remaining initiates seated themselves along the bench, as the moon, now full and more radiant than it had ever been came out from the edge of the earth and rose up into the sky, a vast array of stars shining down with all the sorrows and suffering of the world. The bus took turns along steep ravines, forged paths along roads so narrow they seemed impassable, but my trust was with our driver and my faith with a greater power. I made the sign of the Father, the Son and the Holy Spirit and eased back into my seat, only aware that when I arrived, it would not be at the wrong point in time.

Then, with the Shuar behind them, they began to ingest the foul tea, vomiting and drinking, only reaching out to the heavens for peace of mind and tranquility. The dark grew deep, but no longer with the dread that I once knew, as we made our way through the Andes approaching Riobamba.

The Shuar paced back and forth, urging them to "finish their fate and walk with God." The vomiting continued as the night became divided into millions of pixels, the hum of universe loud and clear. I could see lights in the distance, a shimmering city of lights nestled amongst the mountains. We soon approached the terminal where I had arrived just ten days prior. Not sure of Ana's whereabouts I walked down past the internet café where we had first met, then down to Guayaquil park.

The cold was all-consuming, the initiates still vomiting and wishing for an end, wishing the pain would cease and they could go on living. I walked the pathways, around grass and pond, and then sat on a bench, shivering in the cold, staring down at my own reflection. The voices of all humanity spoke from the depths. Angry words and pretty words. Words that sing and words that dance. Children were being born, then taking those first teetering steps. Young lovers lying in bed, madmen ranting to themselves on city streets, people starving, people dying, people thriving, laughing, loving, smiling.

Then from the shadows came a young woman, walking patiently along the edge of the pond. She stopped at the edge and looked down into the depths, as I got up from my bench and walked over in painful, contracted steps. *The moon rose to its zenith, now small against the sky, as they emptied the remainder of their shells, purging for the final time.*

"Ana?"

"Jack!" she exclaimed, turning in my direction, "You came back!"

"Of course, there was nowhere left to turn."

"I knew you'd come back, my heart told me so."

"Yes, and now we're back where we began and I don't know if I'll ever be able to leave you again."

"Come walk with me," she said as she clutched my hand. "We have all the time we need."

"I will walk with you, but we must walk slowly."

"Are you still in pain?"

"Yes, some, but this is a pain that heals."

"And the other pain?"

"That depends on you."

"You must let go sometime, Jack, and when you do the grace of God will fill your soul, will not leave you frightened and alone. I have faith, you taught me that, and now I must teach you."

And as we walked hand in hand I felt at home. We left the park that night with all the time in the world, still young, still fresh, still mad about each other and hopeful for the human race. We headed back to her truck, back to her home, while hours to the east the ceremony of *Natemamu* had come to an end. *The initiates, drunk out of their senses, stumbled to bed, lying down upon the earth to fall into a long and silent slumber.*

We ate some fruit down in the kitchen, where could be heard hundreds of hungry chickens waiting to be fed. Then up in Ana's bed I pulled down my pants to receive my final shot. She was gentle and told me the bedtime story of the sky and the river and the park. I pulled up my pants and lay still at her side. Then she bent down and turned on music.

"Dance with me, Jack," she said as she crawled out of bed, pulling my hand with all her strength. I took her in my arms as she laid her head on my shoulder. *The night was getting old as the Shuar lay in bed, speaking in a tongue of a time long gone.*

"I watched your favorite movie last night, 'Eternal Sunshine of the Spotless Mind.' It was so beautiful that even when they had lost their memory, they could still be in love."

"The heart is stronger than the mind. When you listen to your heart, not even in death do you depart."

"And did you find your one thing, did you find a way out?"

"You mean, did I find the words for what cannot be described?"

"Yes, tell me Jack, tell me what you found."

"What I found is what I already knew: We die the way we live Ana; death is just a new form of life."

"So, we just go on living for eternity?"

"As you once said, 'A moment is all we have, but as long as we continue the dance, the world will go on living.'"

"And when this song ends, will we continue to dance?"

"If you're willing."

"And when you leave?"

"I haven't left yet."

"You'll come back," she said, "you always will," as she grasped my hand with soft, childlike fingers. *The jungle hummed with the life force of all creation, and as the initiates drifted off into dreams, sick and disoriented. Great laughter echoed in the night and the tongue of an ancient time whispered, "How could they be so silly, how could they forget?"*

"I never did," I thought. "I never did."

ABOUT THE AUTHOR

Timothy studied cultural anthropology and Latin American history at Rutgers College in New Brunswick, NJ and went on to work various temp jobs and backpack his way around the third world. He has written for the magazines Melrose Heights, Tinsel Tokyo, and TCHAD, and We All Dance at Once is his debut novel. He is the co-creator of the website runawaypoets.com and now collaborates with the author and filmmaker Steve Nahaj on video poetry and the Runaway Poets Press. He currently lives and works in his hometown of Princeton, New Jersey.